LAST WILL

a novel by
RON SCHWAB

Poor Coyote Press
PO Box 6105
Omaha, NE 68106
www.PoorCoyotePress.com

ISBN: 1-943421-11-0
ISBN-13: 978-1-943421-11-4

LAST WILL

Dedicated to the memory of Dean Terrill,
journalism teacher extraordinaire,
who always gently suggested,
"Now say the same thing with half the words."

1

Ian

TILLIE CRUMP PLANTED her bare feet in the dusty road, and the determined look on her bulldog-like face told me she had something important on her mind. When Tillie had something to say, you'd just as well resign yourself to listening. She was one tough, old woman, and I would never cross her if I could avoid it.

Tillie, who could be described briefly as short and round, stood like a statue with arms folded over pendulous breasts and waited as I picked up the pace of my morning constitutional around the section. A dozen or more cats of every size and description loitered at her feet, and a few rubbed affectionately against her stumpy legs. Tillie, something of a legend in her time on both sides of the Nebraska-Kansas border, was known locally as the "cat lady," and cats were her life's work.

"Good morning, Mrs. Crump," I said, as I approached, forcing a smile I did not particularly feel at this encounter on a humid, suffocating day. "Looks like another scorcher."

Tillie ignored my neighborly greeting, tugged at the straps of her tattered bib overalls, and limped toward me as I approached.

"We have ourselves a problem, Mr. Locke," Tillie announced

solemnly. We had known each other for better than five years now, but Tillie stood on formality with her lawyer and had long ago disregarded the invitation to address me by my first name.

"Well, Mrs. Crump, perhaps you'd like to drop by the office tomorrow morning, and we can discuss it."

She squinted a porcine eye and sighed with seeming disgust. "It's not my problem, Mr. Locke: it's our problem, and I won't be getting dunned for this."

She was going to have her way with me in a manner of speaking, and I decided I had just as well get on with it. "That being the case, Mrs. Crump, why don't you tell me about our problem, and we'll see if we can solve it?"

She tossed her head in the direction of her farmstead and turned and headed up the rutted wagon path that led to the dilapidated buildings. "You can see it better than I can explain it. It's in the pigpen."

I followed obediently and silently. Tillie was not one for idle chatter, and, despite the public image of my profession, I had determined very early in my career that one never learns much when his own lips are flapping. And I was not that much of a talker anyway.

I walked behind Tillie at half my usual pace, and as we made our way toward our problem, whatever it was, more cats peered through the thick weeds and tangled undergrowth that lined the pathway and began to fall in with the parade. This old woman had a knack for leading me into the ridiculous, and I wondered what she had in store for me this time.

The Pied Piper of catdom had certainly made her mark in Cottonwood County, Nebraska. Horace Crump, the last of Tillie's three husbands, died shortly after I put my shingle out in

Borderview five years earlier, and I settled Horace's estate. Horace had sucked on the barrel of a loaded shotgun and brought himself to a messy end. At least that was the coroner's ruling, the coroner also being the local county attorney, whose medical expertise might be a bit suspect. Some of Horace's friends and neighbors harbored doubts about this version of his demise, speculating Tillie might have played an active role in her spouse's violent exit. Horace had evidently told a neighbor that he had given Tillie a choice—him or the cats. The neighbor had suggested that Tillie chose the felines.

Whatever the truth, Tillie ended up a very wealthy widow, owning more than a section of land, much of it prime river bottom along the Little Blue River southeast of Borderview. No stranger would have guessed her prosperity from her way of life, though, as she resided in a weathering, decaying two-story house capped with a sagging roof that I was certain would not endure another winter. In the course of settling Horace's estate I had entered the dwelling for the first and last time. The cats that shared the house had marked their respective territories throughout and had no sense of propriety about where to deposit their waste. My boots had smelled like cat shit for days after the visit.

As Tillie and I reached the farmyard, we began wading through an ocean of cats, or so it seemed. Certainly, there were well over a hundred of the creatures scattered around the trash-strewn yard, some dozing lazily in the sun, but a good number rushing to greet the company Tillie had brought home. I had nothing against cats, for I admitted to being owned by a cat myself, but a stop at Tillie's always made me sympathetic to any ultimatum Horace may have mistakenly given.

"Over here, Mr. Locke," Tillie said, as she trudged down the slope toward a warped, splintered pen that looked like it might collapse at any moment. Was the pen the problem? Had I been recruited to help with fence repair?

Squealing, grunting hogs greeted us as we approached the over-stocked pen, pressing against the rotting, battered wood panels in near-frenzied expectation of Sunday dinner. They were a mangy bunch, a mix of rangy, tusked boars and bony sows with withered udders. Tillie did not castrate the boars or separate the sexes, and the boars were raked with scars from bloody battles for the trophy of a sow in heat. Tillie had no interest in the finer points of animal husbandry as far as her swine herd was concerned. The cats were her obsession and the hogs were destined for cat food by way of Tillie's meat grinder. The pigpen was mostly wallow, the manure and urine mixing with the soil to form a black gumbo that stuck to the hogs and sucked at their feet, belying the drought that had scorched southeast Nebraska in recent weeks. How sad, I thought, that Tillie's compassion for one species of God's creatures did not extend to these pathetic animals.

"Over there," Tillie said, nodding toward a far corner of the pen where several runts, during the distraction triggered by our arrival, had moved in to feast upon something imbedded in the mud.

I edged around the pen, standing back from the barking, biting snouts that poked through the cracks. Then I saw it. First, a human arm, the flesh stripped nearly to bone. Then Ralph Wainwright's head, bruised and filthy and bloody, with glazed, sunken eyes staring right at me, almost accusingly, from a perch in a V-shaped slop trough some ten feet distant from the naked arm and a scattering of other body parts.

I shook my head in disbelief. "Oh shit, Tillie, why didn't you tell me? What happened here?" I was more than a bit unnerved. I had seen war and the carnage and gore that go with it, but in war you're half prepared for it, and in time, for some anyway, you numb yourself to the slaughter. But this was—or had been—a quiet June Sunday in 1884 far removed in time and place from the battlefields of the Civil War.

"Mrs. Crump, if you please. And I'll ask you to be so kind as to watch your language, Mr. Locke," she said in her Bostonian accent, which I suspected was cultivated, not birthright. "I discovered the intruder when I fed the swine this morning, but I had to look after my kitties before I gave this unpleasantness my attention. I did not invite this man here, and it would please me greatly if you would remove him from my premises. He is a trespasser, you know."

"You do know who this is?" I asked.

"Of course, I do. It's that skinflint banker, Mr. Wainwright, who certainly would have considered himself too high and mighty to grace me with a social visit. Ironic, I should say, that he would meet his end in this place."

My mind raced. Tillie's place was four miles southeast of Borderview, and my small ranch was another mile south of Tillie's. The old woman owned a few draft horses to pull her wagon, but I am not a skilled horseman and I was not inclined to deal with her unruly beasts, so it seemed best that I hightail it home, saddle up my own horse and ride to Borderview for help. The county sheriff needed to be notified immediately about Tillie's discovery.

"We've got to get these hogs away from the body," I said.

"Then I'll get Sheriff Bell out here."

"I just want this man, or what's left of him, off my place before this day is done."

"Well let's see if we can round up a few more panels and fence the hogs away from the remains. Things shouldn't be disturbed any more than they already have been. And for God's sake, we can't let the hogs eat on him anymore."

Tillie turned and plodded at a turtle's pace up the hillside. "Do whatever you need to do, Mr. Locke. This is no longer our problem: it's your problem."

2

Ian

I LEANED BACK in the chair, my feet propped up on the roll-top desk and, from the open window of my second story office, I surveyed the morning activity on the courthouse square across the street. This was more a study of birds, squirrels and other local wildlife, since the courthouse square was just that: a vacant platted square, overgrown with weeds and brush and enclosed by a board fence that helped restrain the goats that were pastured there from time to time to help clean up the vegetation. The county offices and court, for now, were housed in a two-story, brick building on the south side of the square. My own office was perched above a funeral parlor on the west side—a convenient location for a probate lawyer.

TJ leaped on my desk and yowled, sending a stack of carefully organized legal papers floating to the floor—which annoyed me, since in my own mind I am nothing if not organized. "Damn it, TJ, I spent better than an hour getting those things in order. Why can't you be more careful?"

TJ plopped down on his back, and signaled that it was time for a tummy rub. I, of course, obliged. TJ was a yellow tabby cat who had appointed me his servant when he showed up as a frozen, half-starved kitten on the boardwalk outside my office at Christmastime a few years back. I had surrendered to the holiday spirit and treated him to a meal. The rest was history. I named him "Thomas Jefferson Locke"—hence "TJ," and except for occasional absences, which I suspected included romantic interludes at Tillie's cat farm, TJ usually could be found sleeping on the office desk or on the bed at my home. Most days he rode to work with me, wedged snuggly in a saddle bag with his head and front paws sticking out as he surveyed the countryside.

I turned back to the document resting on my lap and re-read it, although I had drafted the thing and pretty much had it memorized:

Last Will of Ralph Wainwright

I, Ralph Wainwright, at this date residing in Cottonwood County, Nebraska, declare this to be my last will and testament, revoking any former wills made by me.

I. I direct that all my just debts and funeral expenses be paid by my executor.

II. I give and bequeath the sum of $1.00 to Celeste Kimball, also known as Celeste Wainwright, to whom I am not, and never have been, married.

III. I give and bequeath the sum of $1.00 to my son, Karl Wainwright.

IV. I give, bequeath and devise all of the rest, residue and remainder of my estate, of whatever nature and kind, to my niece, Emily Stanton.

V. I grant to my executor the authority to administer my estate in his sole discretion and specifically empower him to sell and convey real estate and personal property without court order.

VI. I appoint Ian Locke as executor of this will to serve without bond.

The document had been typed painstakingly by my clerk, Will Heasty, on the Remington typewriter I had brought with me from my former Omaha office—one of only a few such implements in town. It was dated May 10, 1883, slightly more than a year previous, and had been signed by Ralph in his distinctive stilted hand. An attestation clause followed, with signatures of the mandatory two witnesses, Will Heasty and Cash Berry, the undertaker from downstairs.

Celeste was not going to like this, I thought, and I would need to visit her soon. Sheriff Ike Bell had reported that Celeste was properly distraught upon learning of Ralph's demise, but I had known Celeste long before her arrangement with Ralph and was confident she would recover quickly enough from her paramour's death. The estate business would be another matter, and I was particularly uncomfortable with the situation because Celeste and I had kept company in a very serious way at one time. That was before Ralph came along. I did not share the bed of a client's wife or lover—questionable ethics and bad business.

This matter smelled of a nasty squabble, and I had known as much when I drafted the will. Ralph had not explained his reasons for leaving the estate to Emily, a dear friend of mine, but my job was to carry out my client's wishes, and I take great care to avoid even inadvertent influence on the testator who is executing his final farewell.

A soft rapping at my office door interrupted my reverie, and Will, a gangly, bookish, young man with wire-rimmed spectacles, stepped in and pushed the door shut behind him. "Cash Berry's out here, Ian . . . says he's got to see you right now. He's worked up about something."

"Cash is always worked up about something. But send him in."

Momentarily, Cash Berry burst through the doorway, scarlet-faced and wheezing like a blacksmith's bellows. A bald, portly man who, befitting his occupation, always wore a black, vested suit, and today, splotches of perspiration were already seeping through the wool fabric. I rose to greet him and shook his clammy hand. TJ, who had dozed through my conversation with Will, lifted his head and hissed menacingly. He had never cared much for Cash, and Cash still bore a scar on the top of his hand as evidence of the cat's disdain.

"Have a chair, Cash. Will says you've got something important."

Cash plumped down in the chair next to my desk and mopped at his face with a handkerchief. "I've been up to see Celeste about arrangements. She don't seem to give a good goddamn about what's happened to Ralph. Says to do what I want with him. 'Feed the rest of him to the pigs, if I want to,' she says. She ain't exactly a bereaved widow, let me tell you. And she told me to get you up to her place. 'Right now,' she says, and you know Celeste . . . she means 'right now.' I'd be getting up there if I was you."

I sighed. Yes, Celeste was born to command. But I am a bearer of the Locke stubborn streak and do not take well to orders. Celeste could damn well cool her heels for a spell. "I'm going to have some lunch at Reuben's first, and maybe I'll stop by and see Celeste later this afternoon. I need to talk with her anyway."

Cash shifted uneasily in his chair. "It's in your hands now, Ian. I did what I was told, and I'm not responsible if Celeste's pissed at you."

"Celeste is always pissed at me."

"Ian, what am I going to do about a funeral? The widow won't have nothing to do with it. This should have been a big one . . . fancy coffin, full embalming and fixing, even tintypes. Jesus, I brought Ralph back from Tillie's in a gunnysack. I've got most of a skull, one foot, an arm and some loose ribs. Hell, I could bury him in a cartridge box. And Celeste ain't got no interest in sending Ralph off in a way befittin' his station." He paused and looked at me expectantly. "Ian, I witnessed a will for Ralph sometime back, so you must have something to do with settling his estate. Do you reckon you'll be in charge? I'll work out proper arrangements with you . . . at a fair price."

Now we had cut to the real purpose of Cash's visit. I rose from my chair and Cash took the hint. "I'll talk to Celeste," I promised, "and I'll get back to you later."

"It's such an undignified end for a man of Ralph's social standing," Cash lamented, as he moved toward the door.

"I don't think social standing matters much when you're dead. The grave brings total equality, rich or poor . . . white, black, red or yellow."

Cash stopped and turned toward me, looking greatly offended. "That's a morbid way of thinking in my mind, Ian. It matters a lot how you go out. It's the last thought folks have of you. Think about it. If Ralph don't get a proper funeral, what's everybody going to remember about him? That he got ate up by a bunch of pigs . . . low class pigs at that."

Ron Schwab

3

Ian

THE WAINWRIGHT MANSION was perched on a gently sloping hillside just outside Borderview, nearly a mile from the town square, but I opted to walk. It was mid-afternoon now, and I tugged off my coat and soaked in the warmth of the summer sun. I am a warm weather person and rarely complain of the heat and never look forward to our bleak Nebraska winters. My Appaloosa gelding also gave me no incentive to ride. He tended to be contrary during a mid-day saddling and was inclined to bite when annoyed. Hemlock is a mean-looking critter with a splotch of black around one eye that gives him a pirate-like appearance. He's wild-eyed and ill tempered, but a sound horse is a necessity, and I sort of respect his independence. He was a gift from my twin brother, Cam, who could probably take some of the orneriness out of the horse, but his Kansas Flint Hills ranch is nearly a hundred miles south of Borderview.

Cam is a law wrangler, too—that's what some of the old cowboys call those who have taken up the law books. His heart is on the Circle L, a real honest-to-goodness cow and horse operation, unlike my quarter section hideout, but he practices law more than he'd like with the "Judge" in Manhattan, a growing Kansas town not far from Fort Riley. The "Judge" is our father, Myles Franklin Locke, who was an appellate judge in Illinois before he grew bored with life on the bench, pulled up stakes and put out a new shingle on the Kansas prairie. Grudgingly, I must say the Judge has no equal as a lawyer, and his integrity is something to aspire to, but we often butt heads when we get together and it's always worked out best to have some distance between us.

The Locke bloodline overflows with law wranglers. It's like a family curse. My grandfather, William Myles Locke, was a Vermont lawyer, and both of his sons—the Judge and Uncle Nathaniel—were afflicted. Two of Uncle Nathaniel's three children succumbed. My little sister, Hannah, fourteen years younger than I, engages in a struggling practice in Medicine Bow, Wyoming, but baby brother Thaddeus, Hannah's twin, ended up a veterinary surgeon in the Flint Hills. They are issue of the Judge's marriage to Deborah Compton, who died at their birth on July 4, 1855.

My younger brother, Franklin, also escaped the plague, perhaps with divine assistance, and rides a lonely circuit as a Methodist preacher along the Nebraska-South Dakota border. My mother, Sarah McBride Locke, a gentle Quaker woman, had nudged Franklin toward a religious life before her death when he was barely ten, and I often think it would have pleased her greatly to have seen one son shuck off her husband's heathenish ways.

Death has a way of turning my thoughts to family. Does the Judge remain in robust health? Are my brothers doing well? What about little sister? I haven't seen her in three years. When the chips are down, there are few outside of family you can count on, and though I may take a few verbal pokes at the Judge and my siblings and others clinging to the family tree, I don't take such remarks kindly from others. My family, however quarrelsome, is a mighty fortress in times of crisis. Don't take on a Locke unless you're prepared to fight the whole tribe.

Ralph's ghastly end gnawed at me as I made my way up the hill toward his stately home. I had chatted with him amiably at Wainwright Savings Bank Saturday morning. Death strikes once again, unannounced and sudden. The instrument of Ralph's death had obviously been human. With my sons, Ethan and little Cam, disease had dealt the final blow. The result was the same. It was over for all of them. No more tomorrows. We never know if we have more than this moment, and I try to remind myself of that each morning as I check out the sunrise and vow to make the new day count for something.

I would miss Ralph, but I would bear no lingering pain because of his death, and soon he would be no more than a passing thought. I would never get over the loss of my sons, however, and their deaths only three days apart left wounds that could only be understood by one who has lost a child. I wondered if Ralph Wainwright left anyone behind who felt such anguish. Certainly not Celeste.

4

Ian

I WAS ADMITTED to the Wainwright mansion by Greta Kleine, a stocky young German immigrant with short, straw-colored hair and thick calves that peered from her flour-sack dress. I thought her pretty in a fresh, wholesome way, with a flawless, milky complexion and friendly blue eyes that dominated a round face. Greta's father, Gerhardt, was one of the dozens of German farmers who were buying up land in the vast river bottoms that prevailed in the north half of the county. The Germans had invaded, and some of the neighboring communities had taken to referring to Cottonwood County as "Little Deutschland," but that was changing as the Germans started to spill across the borders. They were excellent farmers, hard-working and Lutheran, and they produced children as prolifically as they grew corn and wheat—a sort of slave labor to farm yet more land. Some families farmed as many as two or three quarter sections. The sons worked the land, and many of the daughters, like Greta, worked in the homes of affluent town folks, doing laundry, cooking and other household chores.

"I think Mrs. Wainwright's expecting me," I said.

"*Ja*, I will tell her you are here. She says you are to wait in Herr Wainwright's book room."

"I know the way, Greta. Thank you."

The young woman opened her mouth as if to speak, but then glanced nervously over her shoulder, seemed to think better of it, and moved quickly from the foyer and started up the spiral staircase that led to the bedrooms. She was obviously agitated about something, I thought, but that was not unnatural considering her employer's death, I supposed. I found my way to the library, an elegant, warm room, the only one I envied in this monstrosity of a house that Ralph had built to Celeste's specifications, the result being a sprawling, limestone structure that would have fit nicely on a Southern plantation were it not for the steep roofs and turrets and sharp angles that gave the house something of the appearance of a European castle.

I lowered myself into a stuffed, leather-covered armchair and pulled my watch from my vest pocket. Fifteen minutes till four. Celeste would make her appearance at four o'clock. Every man waited fifteen minutes for Celeste. No exceptions. My eyes scanned the book-lined walls. Political treatises, the works of Shakespeare, all of James Fenimore Cooper's novels, Henry David Thoreau, Nathaniel Hawthorne, Mark Twain, even his recently published Huckleberry Finn, the long awaited sequel to Tom Sawyer. How sad, I thought, that the great books that seduced me from the polished oak shelves were virgins, in a sense, waiting for human touch and love. Celeste had never had any particular interest in books and had been annoyed when they competed for my attention, which was not all that often when Celeste was in the room.

Ralph's reading had been confined to an occasional

newspaper. He was a man of action: a hunter, a horseman, a serious poker player and a more serious drinker. He sought the company of humankind, enjoyed the camaraderie of other men and reveled in the chase of a flirtatious female. No, the books in this house were mere decorations, wasted on creatures who could not possibly love them as they deserved to be loved.

My gaze fastened on a Bierstadt painting, one of the artist's expansive mountain landscapes, when the door quietly opened. I could smell the perfumed fragrance of her before I saw her, and I stood and turned toward the widow Wainwright. She stood in the doorway, her dark, impish eyes betraying her pouty lips. I was welcome, but she was not ready to admit it, and, as always, she nearly took my breath away. She might have been dressed for a ball, wearing a satiny emerald gown, revealing more bosom than proper decorum allowed, her straight raven hair fastened with a ribbon from the same fabric as the gown, and then cascading over her shoulders. She was a very tall woman, only a few inches shorter than I, and I stood a strong six feet two inches. Her smooth, caramel skin strongly suggested strains of Mexican or Indian blood, or perhaps, as some of the good Methodist ladies whispered, African. Few men gave a damn about her origins.

With a haughty toss of her head, Celeste glided toward me and into my arms. Her warm breath caressed my neck, and her lithe body clung to mine as the old heat surged through my own. Her lips found mine, and, for a moment, I responded to her passionate kiss, forgetting the somber purpose of my visit. She had always done this to me, made me absolutely crazy, driven out every sane thought from my mind, leaving me only with the vivid image of our naked, intertwining bodies and the single-minded obsession to bed her.

I stepped back and gently extricated myself from her embrace, and a puzzled look crossed her face.

"I'm sorry about Ralph," I said. "I'll miss him."

Celeste's eyes turned cold and she moved away from me. "I won't," she said. "Ralph had a side that was far different than the one he showed to the town. He had a mean streak no one else ever saw, and it had become worse as he drank more. Frankly, I rarely saw him sober anymore. We no longer shared the same bed . . . or the same bedroom for that matter. It was my choice, not his. I was happy to turn him over to his whores. I can tell you this, Ian, because the bereaved widow act wouldn't fool you anyway. You know that our life was a charade, that Ralph wouldn't marry me and that I stayed with him these past four years for his money, deluding myself that he would eventually do the right thing and make our marriage legal. We were married you know, as far as the town was concerned."

"Yes, Ralph always encouraged the notion that you were man and wife."

The tension between us eased, and we each sought distance from the other, pacing like two trapped pumas on opposite sides of the room. I plucked an untouched volume of Walt Whitman's *Leaves of Grass* from the bookshelves and began thumbing through the pages, recalling that its publishers had been forced to withdraw a new edition from publication a few years back because of charges of indecency. After a moment of uncomfortable silence, I spoke, "I had Ralph's will in my safe. I filed it with the county court clerk before I came over. I haven't petitioned for probate yet. I'm the executor."

"I see."

"It's of record now. I can tell you what's in it."

"I can hardly wait," she said, sarcastically.

"I'm afraid he didn't leave you anything . . . well, a dollar, but that's something lawyers put in to show that disinheritance is intentional."

"Interesting," Celeste replied, apparently nonplussed by the revelation.

"He didn't leave anything to Karl, either."

"Why would he leave anything to that perverted killer? Karl's been sucking Ralph's money teat since he got run out of town. Ralph paid him to stay away. Now it won't matter. I suppose you'll have to notify the little bastard about the will."

"Yes, of course. Anyone with an interest has to get notice."

"That means he'll be back. This is his last chance to strike it rich. He won't take this without a fuss."

"I didn't expect him to . . . you either, for that matter."

She went to the window and pulled back the maroon velvet draperies to let in the sun. She stood there silently looking out onto the oak-studded lawn. The sunlight dropped a soft glow on her profile, and once again I was struck by her sensuous beauty. I undressed her mentally and fought off the urge to join her at the window, sensing that Celeste knew very well the effect she was having on me. She could own me so very, very easily. Celeste had lived a bit shy of thirty years, half the age of her deceased mate, a dozen years younger than I, but she was experienced far beyond her years, intelligent, and, more important for the life she had chosen, extremely cunning. I had no doubt she would survive whatever came her way

She turned away from the window. "So, it's not me. And it's not Karl. So who gets the drunken old fart's estate according to this will of yours."

"It goes to Emily."

"I see. His niece is a slut."

"She's not a slut."

Celeste smiled. "Oh, let's not be touchy." Her scheming eyes probed mine. "You're fond of her, aren't you? You surely can't be sleeping with her. I never thought men would be her cup of tea."

"I'm not sleeping with her," I replied before remembering I owed Celeste no explanation. I placed the book back on the shelf. "I have to go now. I just felt you were entitled to get this information directly from me. I'm glad you're taking Ralph's death so well . . . and this matter of the will."

"I might contest the will."

"You don't have standing. You and Ralph never married. Nebraska doesn't recognize common law marriages, and even if you had grounds . . . which you don't . . . invalidation of the will would mean Ralph died intestate and Karl would end up with everything. You can't even elect to claim a widow's share. I'm sorry."

"No need. The house is in my name. You certainly don't think I'd have moved in with that randy old goat without some kind of security? Of course, there's not a huge market for a home of this quality in Borderview, Nebraska, but it should fetch enough to give me a start should that be necessary. And I've squirreled away a few of Ralph's dollars for a rainy day. I won't be a beggar on the square. But I must tell you, Ian," she said, with a smug look on her face, "I do hold another card."

"Another card?"

"Yes, an ace, to be precise."

I didn't take the bait. She would not be able to resist showing her card.

"You see," she said, "there is another will."

She had snatched my undivided attention. "Another will?"

"Yes, the last will, I believe. Ralph signed it a week ago Sunday. I assume your so-called will was made out before that time."

"More than a year ago."

"Albert Sweeney picked up the will this forenoon. I suspect it's been filed by now, accompanied by my petition for probate."

"Sweeney drafted the will?"

"No, and don't sound so contemptuous when you speak of Albert."

"He's a consensus horse's ass among members of the bar."

"But now he's my horse's ass, and I'll have him treated with respect."

As far as I was concerned, it took the good works of ten lawyers to offset the garbage Sweeney brought down on the profession with his antics. A doughy man with a pencil-thin moustache, Sweeney had a penchant for expensive suits and wealthy widows to buy them. He was a lousy lawyer, but he had prospered via his solicitous charm and nauseating pandering. Why Sweeney, in God's name? Celeste was too smart to be fooled by the likes of that snake.

Celeste moved closer to me, smiling mischievously. "Poor boy. Cat got your tongue?"

I shook my head in disbelief. "So, do you want to tell me about this will?"

"Ralph wrote it in his own hand. Dated and signed. Albert had a fancy name for it."

"Holographic."

"Yes, he said it doesn't require witnesses."

"That's true, but you have to prove the handwriting."

"Albert assured me that wouldn't be a problem."

"May I ask what this purported will provides?"

"I am the sole beneficiary. Albert is named executor."

"Somehow I'm not surprised."

"My, such sarcasm."

I stepped toward the doorway. "I really must go, Celeste. You're represented by counsel, and I shouldn't discuss this with you further. We might be in an adversarial situation here. I have an obligation to speak to Emily about this. It's not a foregone conclusion that your handwritten document will prevail. I'm sure Albert told you there are serious evidentiary burdens to meet in probating holographic wills."

"My, we're sounding like the lawyer now, aren't we? So formal. I'm sorry, Ian, but it's a bit difficult for a woman to take a man seriously when she's seen his bare ass and his honey stick. Don't be condescending with me. I know you inside and out."

I felt myself flushing slightly. "I guess you do, Celeste, but it doesn't change the fact that I do have the responsibility to satisfy myself as to Ralph's true intentions and to get instructions from the person most affected by this turn of events."

I shifted the subject. "Celeste, Cash asked me to talk to you about funeral arrangements. He doesn't realize the ambiguity of your situation. Legally, you don't have any particular authority, but neither does anyone else at this point. Did Ralph ever say anything to you about his wishes?"

A look of disgust crossed her face. "Absolutely not. He hated to discuss anything about death. I think he had convinced himself that death was something that only happened to other people. I'm sure he left no instructions. And since I have no legal responsibility, I want nothing to do with any funeral. You and Cash have my blessing to do whatever you damn well please with the remains of Ralph Wainwright. But before you leave Ian, I must ask you to do something for me."

I studied her suspiciously. "Now what?"

"I would like to have you find me a lawyer."

"What do you mean? You've got a lawyer. You've got Prince Albert."

"He will serve his purpose, but I would like for you to locate someone in Lincoln or Omaha . . . perhaps someone with your old firm would be suitable. I meant something to you once, Ian. Please do this last thing for me. You're the only one I trust to do this."

For the only time I could recall, I saw a trace of fear in Celeste's eyes, a chink in her stonewall of confidence. I knew better, however, than to trust what I saw, as my instincts where Celeste was concerned had a history of being deeply flawed. "You're not making sense," I said. "You have retained legal counsel and now you need another lawyer? What do you want this lawyer to do?"

"I want him to represent me in a very serious matter. A criminal case. You see, by this time tomorrow I expect to be charged with Ralph's murder."

5

Ian

As I OPENED the gate of the wrought iron fence that enclosed the Wainwright yard, I was met by Sheriff Isaac Bell and his young deputy, Jimmy Hawkins, who were hitching their horses to the rail in front of the gate. A somber look clouded a ruddy face that ordinarily would have been dominated by a broad smile and twinkling sky-blue eyes. A bear-like man about my height, but carrying a hundred more pounds, Ike Bell was a displaced cowboy with a gimpy knee, who had carved a new career as a county politician with his amiable disposition and glib tongue. It was next to impossible not to like this genial white-haired man with the ragged, brushy moustache. Ike had a well-honed skill of making almost every man who met him think of him as a good friend. Some of the more refined ladies in the community didn't care for his rough ways, but they didn't have the vote. Still, I always had the feeling Ike was more an actor playing a role than a dedicated lawman, and I suspected he was not above playing fast and loose with the truth if it suited his purposes.

"Good afternoon, counselor," Ike said with his trademark voice that sounded like gravel rubbing on a washboard. "Didn't know Mrs Wainwright had company. Don't see Hemlock tied nearby."

"I walked."

"You need an old cowpoke to help you with that mean-tempered critter, counselor. For a good steak and a few beers, I'd take the cussedness out of him." My reputation as a horseman left something to be desired in our little county.

"I might take you up on that some time, Ike."

Ike spat a stringy brown cud of tobacco, barely missing string bean Jimmy's scuffed boots. Some folks referred to Jimmy derisively as "Ike's pup." The red-haired youngster worshipped Ike like a loyal hound, and his gawky manner and peach-fuzzed cheeks made him look even younger than his twenty years, but I had been told that he could ride a Kansas tornado and shoot the eyes out of a crow in flight—skills not all that critical to a lawman in relatively civilized Cottonwood County, but one never knew.

"Got to ask you something, counselor," Ike said.

"What is it, Ike?"

"You Mrs. Wainwright's law wrangler?"

"As a matter of fact, I'm not."

"Glad to hear that. I'm afraid she's in a passel of trouble."

It was said as an invitation to ask why. Close-mouthed, Ike was not. I obliged. "What kind of trouble?"

Ike turned to Jimmy, who fidgeted nervously. "Jimmy, why don't you head on up to the big house? Wait outside the door till I get there. Just to be sure somebody don't take a notion to leave."

"Yes, sir," Jimmy said, drawing his Peacemaker from its holster and heading through the gate.

Ike called after him. "Jimmy put that damn pistol away. No

sense in getting folks all riled up." He turned to me, shaking his head. "Jimmy's a good boy, but there's a hell of a lot of drying to do behind those ears yet. Thought it best he not hear what I had to say. Boy's got a weakness for gossip and can be a mite loose of tongue."

The pot calling the kettle. "Look, Ike, I've got to be heading back to the office. I'm a bit pushed for time."

Ike leaned back against the hitching post. "You'll want to hear this, counselor. There's some things you might like to know."

"I'm listening."

"I know about the two wills, you see. I was down at the courthouse and heard it in the treasurer's office."

"That's no surprise. News in the courthouse spreads faster than a prairie fire."

"True enough. Let me tell you, old Reuben's about to have a calf over this. He's downright goosey over them two wills. Reuben don't know what he's supposed to do."

Reuben Helvey served as the county judge and also was the proprietor and operator of Reuben's Tavern. He could sign his name and read a bit and carried enough common sense to dispose of the misdemeanors and routine probates and guardianships that were within the jurisdiction of his court. He even looked the part of a distinguished jurist when he donned a black robe, but knowledge of the law or any of its mysteries was not a requirement for getting on the ballot for the part-time job. Reuben had a tendency to go berserk as a rabid skunk when a serious legal issue was dropped on his plate.

"I'm sure Reuben can handle it," I lied.

"Well, anyhow, it don't matter to me. I'm here on more serious business. Afraid me and Jimmy have got to arrest

Celeste."

"Celeste? What in God's name for?" I asked, knowing the answer to my own question.

"Ralph's murder."

"You think Celeste killed Ralph?"

"Sure of it. Got me a witness."

"You're serious?"

"Karl."

"Karl who?"

The sheriff tossed his head and let loose with another slimy wad of tobacco. "Wainwright. Who the hell do you think? Karl's back in town, and he seen it all. Seen Celeste put a bullet in Ralph's brain and seen her throw him to the pigs. The whole works."

6

Ian

When I returned to the office, I found Will Heasty hunched over the typewriter. Will worshipped the typewriter and practiced on it like a virtuoso at the piano, and he was more than proficient, adding a bit of class to the legal documents produced by our office, in sharp contrast to the barely legible, hand-written instruments dispensed by others of the local bar.

My own fascination with the contraption was not so much with the intricacies of its operation, but with my vision of the efficiencies and improvements it could bring to the only tangible product a lawyer could show his client—the written word. When I left my Omaha law firm, I had taken it with me, as a part of the dissolution agreement—my oak desk and the latest model Remington typewriter in the office. It was ironic, I thought, as I watched Will push a crisp sheet of paper into the rubber platen, that E. Remington & Sons, the gun manufacturers, had become the dominant producer of typewriters in the world. Perhaps the pen *was* mightier than the sword, or at least as profitable.

Will was totally absorbed with the work in front of him and had not heard me enter the outer office, so I tapped him lightly on the shoulder. He leaped from his chair, nearly knocking his precious typewriter off the table. "Oh God, Ian, you spooked the hell out of me. I never heard you come in."

"Sorry, Will, but you seemed caught up in your project."

Will brushed back the unruly black hair from his forehead and slipped back into his chair. "I'm working on that contract for the McDowell land that George Washington plans to buy. George wants to put something on McDowell's desk tomorrow. I'll be finished in another hour."

"I appreciate your taking care of that. When George is itching to strike, he gets a little impatient."

"You're always saying, Ian, that the guy on the street who comes to our office doesn't have a notion of whether our work's any good, but he sure as hell knows if we're not getting it done."

"True enough, and if we don't get the work turned out, the client never gets a chance to judge the product anyway . . . and eventually we don't have any clients. Any problems with George's contract I need to know about?"

"No, it's very routine. It could be done on a handshake, if you could trust Clint McDowell to keep his word. George doesn't trust the old fox, though, and probably with good cause."

"I agree." I had total confidence in Will's ability to handle the matter. He was conscientious to a fault, cared about our clients and was a fine wordsmith.

I told Will about the holographic will that had turned up. "It puts a different light on things," I said. "I have to admit this caught me by surprise. I can't imagine Ralph making a new will without speaking with me. I have to ponder our responsibilities here. I guess the final decision is pretty much in Emily's hands. She's the beneficiary of our will. I'm going to catch a train to

Omaha tomorrow to speak with her. I hope to see Mandy while I'm there."

"Do you think Celeste's will is genuine?"

"Who knows? I'd like to have you pull some samples of Ralph's handwriting from his file and go over to the county court and compare it to the holographic will and see what you think. Eventually, if we were going to challenge it, we'd have to find a qualified expert of some kind. On the other hand, it's the proponent's burden to establish validity, so Albert will have to produce some proof of his own. My hunch is that Ralph wrote and signed the will. The larger question is 'why?'"

"I'll be at the county judge's office when it opens in the morning, Ian. I'll try to write out a copy of the will and bring it over to the office to type before you leave for Omaha, so you can have it with you. I've already typed a copy of the other will for Emily."

"I'd appreciate that. I'm going to stay in town tonight. I'm good for supper if you'd like to eat over at Reuben's with me."

Will's face flushed slightly. "Well, I thank you, Ian, but I've got an invitation for later—as soon as I've got this contract finished."

"A supper invitation? It wouldn't be at Elizabeth's, would it?"

Will grinned sheepishly. "Yes, sir."

"She's a fine young woman."

"I'm going to ask her to marry me if I pass the bar examination this fall."

"You'll pass. Have you considered what you're going to do after that? Are you going to head for the big city?"

"Elizabeth would like to stay close to family, I know that. I don't have any living kin that I've ever met, so I'd be happy enough to locate nearby."

"Well, I want you to know there's a place for you here if you want it. This is a growing practice, and I'm ready to take in a partner."

Will beamed and stood up and grabbed my hand and started pumping it enthusiastically. "I don't know what to say."

"I take that for 'yes.'"

"Yes, damn right, yes. You've got yourself a partner." Will finally released his grip on my hand.

"We'll talk about the particulars later, but I'm pleased, Will. I think this can be a good decision for both of us." I was delighted with the prospect of Will remaining with the law office. He had a high school diploma, which was more formal education than most Western lawyers had, and he had started absorbing his knowledge of the law and its sometimes bizarre workings as a clerk "reading the law" in the office of old Cyrus Flowers, who had started winding down his practice a few years previously and had prevailed upon me to take Will in. Cyrus had said we would be a good fit, and, as usual, he had been right.

I heard TJ yowling from behind my office door and walked over to let him out.

"Oh, I almost forgot, Ian," Will said, as he sat back down at his typewriter. "Be sure to check your desk. There's a Western Union from Omaha."

7

Ian

I LAY NAKED on top of the scratchy sheets that covered my bed in the Fremont Hotel. TJ snoozed nearby on the windowsill, claiming first rights to any breeze that might find its way into the steamy room. The glow of a full moon sifted through the filmy curtains, and I did not need the oil lamp to skim the pages of Mark Twain's latest effort, *The Adventures of Huckleberry Finn*, especially since my eyes stared at the pages without seeing the words.

The telegram had been sent by the former Mrs. Locke, now Nadine Hampton. Simple, but ominous, words: MUST SEE YOU IMMEDIATELY. STOP. NADINE. STOP. My immediate reaction had been momentary panic—something had happened to our daughter, Amanda. After a brief dialogue with myself, I was somewhat reassured. All messages I received from Nadine carried terse, urgent tones and were laced with mystery. She had always had a flair for the dramatic, and she was a bright, perceptive woman with a keen instinct for getting one's attention. After a dozen years of marriage, she had me pretty much on a neck rein and knew what gentle yank would yield what result.

She was sleeping soundly this night, confident I was tossing in my bed, stewing about her summons, certain I would be in Omaha by nightfall tomorrow. And, of course, I would verify her confidence. Tomorrow morning, I would leave TJ at the office, since Will had offered to look after him during my absence. Then, after a brief stop at the county jail, I would purchase a ticket for the ten o'clock train and embark on the sweltering journey to the growing metropolis of thirty thousand souls on the Missouri River.

I pay monthly rent for a room at the Fremont and maintain a modest wardrobe there, as my work seduces me too many late nights, and it is often easier to drop in the hotel bed than to saddle up a cranky horse and make the half-hour ride out to the ranch house. I love the isolation and open spaces there, but I can't savor them much when the hour approaches midnight. Fortunately, my best friend and neighbor, George Washington, looks after my cow herd, which only numbers about forty cows with calves at side, and keeps an eye out for any trespassers. George even checks in with TJ when I leave him in charge of operations, usually depositing a fresh catfish yanked from the nearby Little Blue for his culinary pleasure. TJ considers George a friend, too.

Yes, his name is George Washington. In another life he was called Walking Turtle. He is a full blood Pawnee of about sixty winters, as the Indians might say, and his senior wife's name is Martha. I say this seriously. I refer to Martha as the senior wife, because George has two other "wives," but Martha, who is closer to George's age, was his "First Lady," as he puts it, and is his official emissary to Cottonwood County society, such as it is. When we were sharing an evening of tall tales and whiskey in front of the fireplace at my home a few winters back, George shared with me the origins of his name. He had learned about the first of the Great White Fathers at a Quaker school he attended as a boy and had been totally fascinated with the career of the great man. Warrior, farmer, President. When he decided to walk the white man's trail, he believed he should adopt a white man's name, and since the first George Washington had no children, the former Pawnee scout decided to give him a namesake. There may be some truth to this, but I would not be surprised to hear another version pass George's lips on some future winter evening. He plays a little loose with the truth sometimes. And I would trust him with my life.

George Washington is also one of the wealthiest men in the county. If he acquires the McDowell half section, his acres of farm and grassland will tally over two thousand. He trades heavily in furs and operates a limekiln that produces building stone that is shipped to four states. His two eldest sons, married to German sisters, manage most of the enterprises these days, but George's empire will have places for the ten younger children as they come of age. George devotes his energies increasingly to his oil painting, the avocation of his heart. He is an accomplished artist, and I treasure the painting of a nude Indian maiden that hangs on the wall of my home study—and bears an amazing likeness to George's youngest wife. I should advise that I use the term "wife" euphemistically. The laws of the sovereign state of Nebraska, of course, do not bless polygamy, but no one seems to care much about George's living arrangements. He is an honest man, who has always worked hard, and his dollars support many local families. Social outrage seems to dissolve in the face of such achievement.

My thoughts turned involuntarily to Celeste. She was incarcerated in the county jail, and she would be in a rage when I visited her tomorrow morning—a visit I would much prefer to avoid. I needed to confirm, however, that she still wanted me to seek legal counsel in Omaha. The whole situation was a bit messy ethically, since Celeste was technically an adverse party with respect to the will dispute, and it was important that I extricate myself from the situation as soon as possible. There was an unhealthy bond between us that would not let me walk away and wash my hands from her dilemma—even if it was one of her own making. As a lawyer, her guilt or innocence was not the issue. She was entitled to the full protection of the law, and I felt an irrational responsibility to help her get it. Personally, I was baffled. Was Celeste capable of murdering Ralph? I decided that Celeste was, indeed, capable of doing about anything. Ralph's death after making a holographic will, if in fact he had, was certainly convenient timing from Celeste's standpoint. And still, it all seemed too simple. I would have expected Celeste to find a more devious route to Ralph's wealth.

Then there was the matter of Karl Wainwright. To my knowledge he had not returned to Borderview for at least five years, having departed shortly after what locals referred to as the "Oakley thing." I had never met the young man, who would be in his early thirties now, but Cy Hamilton had told me once that Karl was a suspect in the unsolved rape and murder of a twelve-year old farm girl, Rachel Oakley. Her brutalized body had been found on the edge of the county fairgrounds following a visit by a traveling carnival, and, at first, Ike Bell had been convinced that someone from the carnival company had perpetrated the unspeakable acts. Later, however, witnesses had attested to seeing

Karl hovering around the girl at the county fair. He had purchased treats for the girl and given her prizes he won at some of the carnival games. It had all seemed innocent enough at the time, but some folks wondered after the girl's tragic death. Ike had not found a direct link to Karl and the girl, and one didn't arrest the son of a wealthy, popular banker on the basis of rumors. Karl discreetly disappeared and the outrage died quickly. It was interesting that Karl had returned to Borderview only a few days before his father's murder. I was curious about this man and had no doubt our paths would cross soon enough.

8

Ian

THE ENGINE BELCHED smoke and the whistle screamed mournfully as the train approached Omaha. I straightened up in my seat, jolted from the sleep to which I had been lured by the combined effects of the warm sun streaming through the windows and the monotonous clanking of steel against steel. I was still mildly apprehensive about Nadine's message, and the stately Hampton residence would be the first stop. Events had dovetailed to give this mission multiple objectives, however.

I had wired Emily Stanton at the *Omaha Bee*, where she was a crime reporter, and informed her I would be dropping by her boarding house this evening. She should have received yesterday's message about her uncle's death, but she knew nothing about the multiple wills, or that she was named a beneficiary of one of the instruments, and I wasn't certain what her reaction would be. As the beneficiary in the will I had drafted, her instructions would determine how vigorously I would pursue probate of that document.

Tomorrow, I would need to search out a criminal lawyer for Celeste. My former firm catered to clients in the world of commerce and tended to keep crimes of violence at a distance. Fraud and deception might fit under the umbrella of *Gray and Dawson*, formerly *Locke, Gray and Dawson*, but most certainly not murder. Charlie Gray would likely have some thoughts on a lawyer who would take on the case, though. In any event my visit with Celeste in her bleak cell at the county jail had been businesslike and matter of fact. Celeste complained only a bit about the accommodations and seemed composed, almost serene, and, yes, I was still conscripted to procure legal counsel, after which she understood my responsibilities to her would be terminated.

First, however, I had to face Nadine. Not a pleasant thought. The other side of that coin, however, was the opportunity to see my precious Amanda, and I brightened at the prospect of a visit with my daughter. I recalled without pleasure the bitterness and meanness of our divorce. It was hard to understand how two people who had once loved each other so fiercely could find so little redeeming in the other when the final break came. I suppose our marriage had started to crumble after we lost the boys in the winter of 1874. The diphtheria scourge had swept the country that year, wiping out entire families in some instances, leaving others with voids that would never be filled, and the Lockes, with all their money and prestige, had not been spared. Ethan and Cam had been rambunctious, bright and happy boys, frolicking in the snow as January waned. A week later, they were gone. Amanda, still a year-old suckling baby, had been untouched.

I failed as husband and father after the boys died. I turned first to my work, keeping still longer hours at the office. Somehow, I was always able to function there in that other world beyond the family, and I must say that my productivity as a lawyer never suffered, not in the slightest. At home, though, the whiskey bottle became my companion in the stillness and loneliness of the night, and I was of little comfort to Nadine, who seemed to be stronger and more resilient than I. Perhaps, it was her daily responsibility for our remaining child that kept her sane. She also had a bevy of friends who visited regularly and shared her life, giving her the support she did not receive from a morose husband who was so caught up in his own grief, he abandoned those who shared his loss. My only respite came when I cradled tiny Amanda in my arms. Finally, Nadine asked me to leave. I complied.

Nadine and I lived apart for two years before she filed a petition for divorce, alleging adultery as grounds. I did not contest the divorce; on the contrary, I welcomed it. By this time I was ready to bring some order to my life, and Amanda seemed to be about all Nadine and I had in common anymore. At first I was outraged when I learned that Emily had been named as the correspondent in the divorce proceedings, as there had never been that kind of romantic intimacy between us. On the other hand, we had been dear friends for a several years, and during my estrangement from my wife, we shared many evening dinners where she endured my nightly descent into the abyss of self-pity. Emily persuaded me to leave well enough alone. To challenge Nadine's allegations would only draw attention to the case, and without grounds stated there could be no divorce, she observed.

I capitulated totally on the issue of Amanda's custody, although there was significant court precedent in Nebraska upholding the principle that children are a father's property and that he has an absolute right to their services. The doctrine was starting to fall out of favor, however, and at that time in my life I questioned my qualifications as a father, and I did not have it in me to put a four-year-old child in the middle of a battle that was not of her making. I had come to regret this surrender, but life is about choices and living with the decisions we make and doing the best we can on that path we chose at the fork in the road.

9

Ian

NADINE AND I sat in the sitting room of Hampton Manor, as some of the natives called the imposing Victorian house owned by the heir presumptive to the Hampton meat packing empire. She presided with regal grace over the teapot that the maid had deposited on the tea table, and I noted that the years had been kind to her. Her hair might have been spun gold, and she was still slender as a reed. Only the creases carved lightly in the pale flesh around her striking blue eyes suggested that she was nearer forty than thirty.

"Your telegram suggested urgency," I said. "Is Mandy alright?"

"I truly wish you would refer to our daughter by her given name. Amanda is quite fine."

"I'd like to spend some time with her before I leave."

"She won't be home from the academy until late. The young ladies have special violin instructions after classes. You will see her tomorrow, I assure you."

"Mandy plays the violin?"

"And the piano. She's extremely talented. Professor

Steinkraus thinks she may be a prodigy."

"I had no idea."

"No, you barely know the child. I'm sure you wouldn't."

"I make a trip to Omaha to see her every month. I make plans, and she's never here. I've seen her only three times in the past year, but you know as well as I that it's not for lack of trying. I telegraph you a week before I come, but you never reply. You always refuse when I ask to arrange a visit to my ranch. This is a tiresome game, Nadie, and it's wrong." She winced at my use of her pet name. It was not always so. I know it annoys the hell out of her, and I won't deny this may motivate me.

Nadine bit her lower lip, as she always did when she was trying to get a grip on her anger. She appeared uncharacteristically edgy, certainly not her usually calm and controlled self. Her demeanor, in turn, made me nervous. I fought at Gettysburg, but there was little ambiguity in that battle, a simple matter of kill or be killed. Nadine and I carried on a wounding and maiming type of war, more in the nature of guerilla conflict—hit and run—and I doubt that any impartial observer would have seen particular nobility on either side of the fray. This war honored neither of the combatants.

"Are you still drinking?" Nadine asked.

"What in the hell kind of question is that?"

"I am willing to give you an opportunity to become acquainted with your daughter. But I don't want to endanger her."

"Endanger her? You're addled, Nadine. You've never seen me commit an act of violence against anyone . . . man, woman or child."

"No, I'm not suggesting you are a violent man now, but your

history says you are capable of violence. I'm more concerned about moral endangerment. I don't want my daughter under the care of a drunk."

"I don't know what this is all about. I'm not a drunk, and I don't think I ever crossed over that line. I admit I drank too much the last few years of our marriage, but I was never out of control. Anyway, I have only an occasional drink now and don't have much of a taste for the stuff anymore. As for violence, I was a soldier, Nadine, for God's sake."

"What kind of living accommodations do you have at your ranch for a young lady?"

Nadine's interrogation seemed to promise the possibility of a carrot at its conclusion, and I decided instantly to play this little game by her rules. "I have an extra bedroom. It's a small home, but very well built and comfortable. My friend, George, constructed most of it from native limestone. If you're suggesting Mandy . . . Amanda . . . might visit, I think it would be a wonderful experience for her. She loves horseback riding, and George would help her select a horse from his herd . . . my judgment of horseflesh being dubious. We're nearing the end of calving season now, and she'd get a kick out of the new babies."

Nadine rolled her eyes and sighed. "I don't think Amanda would be much interested in your smelly cows, but that's unimportant. I'm more concerned about other matters. Do you have schools?"

"You're serious? Borderview just built a new high school. There's a grade school just a mile from the ranch, and since I go to town every day, Amanda could go to the school there if she wanted. Borderview is a railroad town. Civilization has arrived, more or less. Are you suggesting Amanda might come for a long stay?"

She did not answer my question. "I'm very concerned about her music. She is gifted. I want her to have opportunities to cultivate her gift."

"We do have a woman in town, who I am told once performed professionally and gives private piano lessons. I believe she has the ability to play and teach other instruments as well." I hoped it was not too deceitful to omit from the resume that Claudette Beard's professional experience had been as a dancer-piano player in a Lincoln saloon and that her other instruments were the banjo and harmonica—the latter instrument which she could play with her nose—or that she was a colored lady. I would not call Nadine a Negro hater, but she had her notions about where certain races belonged in society's pecking order.

Nadine narrowed her eyes and studied my face. I had given up occasional white lies early in our marriage—I'm a terrible liar, and out of practice anyway—but I could sometimes get away with stretching the truth just a bit. She decided to give me a pass on this one.

"Victor and I are planning to travel to Europe. The Hamptons have business interests there, and Victor insists that I accompany him. We may be out of the country for six months or more and will not be in a single location long enough to enroll Amanda in school." I found her remarks strange since the Hamptons could easily afford to employ a private tutor to accompany them on the trip, but I was not about to point out the obvious.

"I assume you're asking if Amanda can stay with me while you're out of the country. The answer is 'yes.' I would love to have her."

"You should be warned, Ian, that Amanda is not going to like this one bit. I have discussed this with her, and she insists she will not go with you to Borderview."

"Are you giving her a choice?"

She was silent for a moment. Tears welled up in her eyes and one rolled down her cheek. Perhaps this once warm, carefree woman had not turned to stone after all. "No, she has no choice. Her things are packed. You will need another ticket for tomorrow afternoon's train. I don't want you to come here. I will bring her to the station promptly at one o'clock."

10

Ian

I WAITED PATIENTLY in the immaculate parlor of the boarding house, savoring the aroma of baking bread that drifted in from the kitchen. When I had shown up at the door shortly before dusk, I was met by the buxom landlady who reminded me of a well-fed pigeon poised to peck my eyes out. I had undergone my second interrogation of the day before the woman had consented to inform Emily of the arrival of a gentleman caller. Thereafter, she had disappeared up the stairway, mumbling to herself between heavy sighs.

I felt a special kinship with Emily, although it was one of those things I could not convert to precise words. Our relationship had never edged close to romance, although I was keenly aware that she was a striking woman who would catch a second look from any observant male—even though she did nothing to encourage it. She seemingly tried to hide her appearance with high-necked dresses and wide brimmed hats that tended to shield her dark, intelligent eyes and smooth olive skin. Books and words were our bond, and we had shared many hours engaged in serious and intense debate about the works of

Emerson, Thoreau, Twain, Hawthorne, Shakespeare, and other writers who had made their marks in the world of literature. She earned a meager living as a reporter, but she aspired to be a novelist, which would likely earn her even less. It had occurred to me that an inheritance from Ralph might afford her the freedom to pursue her dream.

I heard footsteps on the stairway and got up from my chair just as Emily Stanton rushed through the doorway and into my arms, squealing with joy. "Ian, Ian, it's been too long."

I hugged her tightly for a moment before she kissed me softly on the cheek and slipped from my embrace. The landlady had followed Emily and stood at the foot of the stairs, arms folded and a scowl on her face. Emily turned quickly to her and said, "Mrs. Schopf, this is my dearest friend in the whole world, Ian Locke. Ian, this is my landlady, Mrs. Schopf."

"We've met," she replied coolly. "Remember the rules. There will be no entertaining of gentlemen in the private rooms." She stomped into the kitchen.

"I don't think she likes me," I said.

"Mrs. Schopf has little use for men. She had a husband who caught the wanderlust years back and headed west to the goldfields, leaving Mrs. Schopf with a brood of children to raise. She never heard from him again. Now, enough of Mrs. Schopf. You didn't make this visit to discuss my landlady." Emily took my hand and led me to a stuffed sofa. "We have so much to talk about."

I sat down beside her. "We do have a lot to discuss. Perhaps we can catch up a bit, and then I can take you to dinner."

"I've already made reservations at The Castle. You're my guest tonight. We're due there in an hour and a half . . . eight o'clock sharp. A friend of mine is meeting us there . . . I hope that's all right. I really want you to meet this person."

"A friend? A beau, perhaps?"

She tapped my arm gently and gave me a look of feigned exasperation. "Not a beau. A friend. Casey McGlaun. A lawyer, of all things."

"You know I really don't care much for lawyers. They're stuffy and boring and so full of themselves."

"I don't find you stuffy and boring . . . although on occasion you can be a bit full of yourself."

I smiled. "You've always had good taste in lawyers, I must admit. I look forward to meeting your Mr. McGlaun."

"You'll find Casey very interesting. I promise."

"Well, if we have an engagement for dinner, we'd better get down to business. I need some instructions from you about your Uncle Ralph's will."

"Instructions?"

"Yes. You see, Ralph left a will naming you his sole beneficiary."

Emily's eyes widened. "Me? You're joking, of course."

"I couldn't be more serious."

"But what about Karl . . . and Celeste?"

"Not a nickel, but there are complications—there appears to be another will."

I pulled Will Heasty's typewritten copy of the will I drafted for Ralph out of my coat pocket and handed it to Emily. "My clerk typed up an extra copy of the will for you. You can see for yourself. I'm executor, but what I do about it depends on some decisions you have to make.

I went over the terms of the two wills with Emily and told

her about Celeste's arrest for Ralph's murder and of Karl's sudden appearance in Borderview, as Emily listened in stunned silence. When I completed my narrative, she shook her head in disbelief.

"I don't know what to say. It's like some kind of bizarre novel."

"It's a strange story alright, and you have to help write part of it."

"I never expected an inheritance from Uncle Ralph . . . I don't want any. I truly loved him. Mother said he was something of a rogue and she disapproved mightily of his relationship with Celeste. But before she died last year, she made me promise I would stay in touch with him . . . and I did. I wrote to him at least once a month, although he wasn't much of a letter writer himself. He always took time to look me up whenever he came to Omaha, and he saw Mother frequently before her death. He paid for her funeral. He was always kind to us . . . and generous to Mother. She had very little in the way of worldly goods and might have been a pauper were it not for her brother. I can only judge a man by how he treats me and mine, and by that standard he was a good man. He was the only family I had left, unless you count Karl . . . and I do not."

"So do you want me to pursue probate of the will?"

"What does 'pursuing it' mean?"

"It will mean challenging the holographic will in court. If that will is ruled valid, the will I drafted is null and void. The most recent will prevails. On the other hand, the courts have consistently ruled that a murderer . . . in this case, an alleged murderess . . . cannot benefit from the death of the victim. The provision in the will for Celeste would be invalid if she should be found guilty. The question then becomes one of whether the holographic will revoked the earlier will or whether that will is revived by failure of the second will's provision. If the court rules that the earlier will was revoked, then the estate would be distributed under the laws of intestate distribution."

"Intestate distribution?"

"Lawyer talk for dying without a will. If you don't have a will, Nebraska statutes set forth a scheme for distributing the estate to the next of kin. Ralph had a son, and the laws of intestate distribution would give him the entire estate."

"Do you have any idea how confusing all of this is?"

I squeezed her hand gently. "That's what law wranglers like myself do, my dear friend. We try to create some order out of chaos."

Emily was dubious. "I'm not interested in making a fuss. I did nothing to earn an inheritance. I've managed to make my own way without it, and I never had any expectation of such a windfall. It seems to me that I could best reduce the chaos by declining to be involved. What do you advise?"

"It seems to me, legal issues aside, the goal should be to carry out Ralph's intent. The problem, of course, is that his intent is a bit murky at the moment. I know that he was very emphatic about his wishes when I made out his will . . . he wanted you to inherit his estate. He knew I kept the will in my safe, and he never asked me to return it or destroy it. As to the holographic will, there has to be an explanation. First, we cannot be entirely certain it is his handwriting. My clerk, Will Heasty, is looking into that question and may have some thoughts when I get back to the office. I don't think there's any basis for setting the will aside on grounds of incompetency of the testator . . . as near as I know, Ralph was of sound mind. He had been nursing the whiskey bottle regularly the last year or so, according to town gossip, and I suppose he could have written the will when he was blind drunk . . . but I didn't see any hint of that in the wording of the will or in the steadiness of the hand that wrote it."

"It doesn't appear to me there is much basis to contest this will even if I were inclined to do so."

"Undue influence is another possible ground."

"What does that mean?"

"The will could be set aside if there was evidence that he wrote the will involuntarily . . . under threat of blackmail, for instance. Or, perhaps, someone held a gun to his head, not just a remote possibility in light of the way Ralph met his maker."

"But we have no proof."

"Not yet, but much of the story remains untold. These things have a way of coming to light. And Will and I can do some digging of our own. Take my word for it. Ralph Wainwright did not want Celeste to end up with his estate, or Karl either, for that matter. If you walk away from this, one or the other finds the pot of gold."

Emily's eyes narrowed and she bit her lower lip softly as she pondered the situation. After a long silence she finally spoke. "If I should come into some money, I guess I don't have to keep it all. I can use it for worthy causes. The suffrage movement is in great need of funds, and I have always wanted to help the Children's Home."

"You would have the right to call off the dogs at any time if you were not comfortable with the direction the case was going. If we learn the truth and it contradicts what I presently believe to be true, I would encourage you to back off."

"It makes me feel very greedy somehow just to be thinking about this. How much time do I have to make a decision?"

"Not much. As the named executor, I've already directed Will to file a petition for probate. Another petition has been filed for probate of the holographic will. I anticipate that Judge Helvey will bring the petitions up for hearing simultaneously, but I don't think he'll want to commit to a decision until he sees what happens with the murder charges against Celeste. We could use time for investigation anyway, so I would try to get a continuance of the hearing and ask that I be appointed special administrator until some disposition is made of Celeste's case.

"What's a special administrator?"

"A person appointed by the court to manage estate assets until a will is actually admitted to probate. It's a temporary job, so to speak. But the special administrator has most of the powers of an executor and has a responsibility to compile and file an asset inventory with the court. At the moment, no one has authority to manage and take charge of Ralph's financial holdings, and if you say 'go' I'm inclined to seek immediate appointment."

"Can you be certain the judge will appoint you?"

"No, but we'd make a darn good try. Prince Albert will squeal like a pig and put forth his own entitlement. Reuben . . . Judge Helvey . . . tends to wither under fire and might appoint a third party. That would be my fall-back position."

Emily smiled wryly and turned to me and brushed my cheek lightly with her fingertips. "You already have your battle plan don't you?"

I shrugged and grinned sheepishly. "I can't help myself. But you're the commander-in-chief. You say 'no' and the war's over."

Emily stood up and paced the room for some minutes.

Silences were never uncomfortable between us, and I waited patiently until she sat down beside me and clasped my hand in both of hers, her dark eyes fixed directly on mine. "The commander-in-chief says 'yes.'"

11

Casey

THE YOUNG WOMAN stood silently in the entryway to the expansive dining area of The Castle, half hidden by a suit of armor that was posted like a menacing guard adjacent to the wide opening. The casual observer might have taken note of a coltish girl who appeared ten or more years younger than her thirty. Her long auburn hair gleamed like polished copper in the flickering glow of the gas-lighted room and cascaded loosely over her shoulders. A sprinkling of freckles swept across the bridge of her nose and faded into a flawless complexion that accentuated intense, green-flecked brown eyes. Without her pumps, she stood little more than five feet tall, but her slender frame and confident bearing gave an illusion of greater height, and the second look that inevitably came her way revealed a stunning woman whose serious demeanor invited no more than that extra look.

Her eyes were fixed on a man and woman who sat at a table in the far corner of the room against a background of shields and axes and other weapons that adorned the walls that carried out The Castle's medieval theme. She had recognized Emily Stanton instantly, but it was Emily's companion who warranted her studied gaze, and she was giving herself the edge of first appraisal.

He was a lean man, and from the long legs that were tucked uncomfortably under the dining table, she judged he was quite tall. His thick, sandy hair appeared to be salted with gray at the temples, and she guessed he could be a year or two on either side of forty. Emily uncharacteristically seemed to be carrying the brunt of the conversation, while her companion listened attentively with a rather grim look on his face. An old sourpuss, although a rather handsome one. Emily generally had interesting friends, and even from a distance she sensed a certain presence in the stranger that intrigued her.

The woman straightened her hair, stepped out of the shadows and moved briskly toward the couple. As she approached the table, Emily caught a glimpse of her, waved and smiled broadly and rose to meet her. The tall man stood also, and she caught a quizzical look on his face as the women hugged brief greetings. Emily turned to the man, who was quite tall as she had guessed, perhaps several inches over six feet.

Emily said, "Mr. Ian Locke, may I present Miss Casey McGlaun?"

Locke seemed momentarily bewildered at the mention of her name and shot a quick look at Emily, but recovered quickly and accepted Casey's extended hand. "My pleasure, ma'am. I've heard very complimentary words about Casey McGlaun, and I generally . . . with a notable exception or two . . . consider Emily a reliable purveyor of truth."

Locke's steel-gray eyes fixed on Casey's longer than mere politeness might dictate and she met his gaze unflinchingly. Faint traces of a smile formed on his lips, and in spite of his taciturn face, his eyes glinted with amusement. There was a private joke here that she was not privy to.

Emily interrupted the stare-down. "I'm starving. Let's sit down and order."

Locke seated the ladies and took his own chair. The women sat on each side of Locke so that the diners formed something of a triangle at the round table. All three ordered steaks with fried potatoes. Emily and Casey each had a glass of red wine, and Locke settled for a cup of black coffee. Their conversation was polite and mundane while they ate. Emily could not finish her steak and offered the healthy remains to her friends. Locke declined, so Casey shrugged and shifted the uneaten meat to her own plate, realizing this was not proper etiquette in polite society. She reminded herself that where she came from, one ate when the opportunity presented, because you never knew when the next meal might turn up. To hell with polite society. Locke passed on dessert, but Casey devoured a huge slice of apple pie. After dinner, the waiter brought coffee for the women. Casey sipped from her steaming cup before she set it down and announced abruptly, "The two of you are my guests this evening."

"But I invited you and Ian as my guests," Emily protested.

"I won a case yesterday . . . a paying one, believe it or not. Douglas County District Court. My client was so thrilled, she paid me my twenty dollar fee on the spot."

Locke leaned forward, obviously interested. "A jury trial?"

"No, it was a bench trial before Judge Wallman."

"I know Wallman. He's a good judge . . . controls his courtroom and very fair."

"It was a simple case . . . breach of contract. My client is a seamstress with several employees working in her home. The owner of a mercantile store had agreed to buy a large quantity of shirts at a set price from my client, but after she produced the shirts, he reneged. As a matter of fact, he found a wholesaler who could provide inferior merchandise more cheaply. I was blessed with a smart client. She had obtained a signed letter from the defendant confirming the order before she began production. I took the case with the understanding there would be no fee if I lost, but I was to be paid twice my usual fee if I won . . . double or nothing you might say. Not a glamorous case, but very satisfying."

"Do you handle many criminal cases?" Locke asked.

"That's about all I do. I represent mostly women in civil matters . . . not necessarily by choice . . . and a good number of criminals of both sexes who cannot afford the fees of the more prominent male lawyers," she said matter-of-factly.

"How long have you been practicing?"

"A little more than three years. I graduated from Denver University, then moved to Omaha at Emily's urging, passed the bar exam and put out my shingle here."

"She's been very successful," Emily interjected. "Casey's building a serious reputation among the criminal bar."

"Omaha is a good place to start a practice," Locke said. "There aren't near enough lawyers here to meet the demand, and there's a growing moneyed clientele for the right lawyers to tap. There's plenty of work in our small towns, but not enough money. One of my former partners warned me when I decided to leave Omaha that he'd never known a country lawyer who got rich practicing law. He said if you encounter a wealthy country lawyer, find out what his sideline is and that's where you find the source of his prosperity. Of course, a rich wife can't hurt any." Locke smiled wryly. "Unfortunately, I have neither profitable sideline nor wealthy wife."

"And the money's not important to you?"

"Oh, I like a dollar as well as the next man, but I want to earn it on my own terms. The lower overhead in a place like Borderview gives me a bit more leeway in choosing the work I do, and I get great satisfaction out of representing clients I know personally, and, for the most part, like. I'm a capitalist, and I face the reality of earning a living, but I no longer forget to nurture the spirit, so to speak. Where I live and what I do with my time on this earth is important to me. Other people own less of me in Borderview than they did when I practiced in Omaha."

Casey studied Locke's face intently. "You might make an interesting subject."

"Subject?"

Emily intervened. "Casey's very taken with psychology."

"The science is in its infancy now, but I read everything I can find about it. We know so little about the human mind. But someday we're going to know a lot. I wrote some articles about a German psychiatrist, Sigmund Freud . . . fascinating man. A little crazy himself, though, I think. Understanding why people do what they do can be invaluable to a lawyer . . . or anyone, for that matter."

Locke was silent, and Casey could feel his appraising gaze. Oddly, he did not make her feel self-conscious. There was something about him that loosened her tongue.

Emily let the silence linger, and sipped at her coffee before speaking. "Casey and I met when we were both writing for the McClure syndicate out of Denver. Sidney McClure sent Casey all over the country on writing assignments nobody else wanted to handle. When there was rioting in a mining camp at Cripple Creek, Colorado a few years back, the troublemakers threatened to lynch any newspaperman who showed up. McClure sent a newspaperwoman instead. Casey filed regular reports under her byline, but nobody in the camp ever guessed that 'Casey' was a woman."

"How did you keep from being found out?" Locke asked.

Casey flushed slightly and smiled sheepishly. "I camped with the prostitutes. The women didn't ask any questions as long as I didn't compete for their business, and the men assumed that a woman wouldn't have any other purpose there. My living arrangements inspired another series of articles."

"How did you end up in law school?"

"I enjoyed the action more than the writing, and during my newspaper days, I noticed that wherever there was a controversy, lawyers always seemed to end up in the middle of it. My father was a Cavalry sergeant, and I was raised on army posts in Texas and Arizona. I even survived several attacks by *Coyotero* Apaches when dad was posted at Fort Apache. It must be the army in my blood. That's why I became a lawyer. I like to be in the thick of the fight. I suppose that's why I thrive on trial practice. I would never make an office lawyer."

"And I'm not cut out to be a trial lawyer," Locke said. "I'm more peacemaker than warrior."

"But you have fought. Emily said you were at Gettysburg . . . that you were a major. Cavalry?"

"Infantry. A brevet major. A kid promoted on the battlefield because everybody up the chain of command was dead or dying." He spoke very softly and his face turned grim. She had obviously touched a raw spot.

Casey noted that Emily deftly came to the rescue. "Ian, you might be interested to know that Casey's only the second woman admitted to the bar in Nebraska . . . and the first woman law school graduate. Ada Bittenbinder was the first admitted, but she read the law under her husband's tutelage and was admitted by examination."

Locke commented, "Ada's made a reputation for herself. She's the attorney for the National Women's Christian Temperance Union. And she's one of only a few women admitted to practice before the United States Supreme Court. Not many male lawyers can claim that distinction."

"And," Emily added, "now she's talking about being a candidate for Nebraska Supreme Court Judge. Of course, she won't be able to vote for herself. And neither will two of us at this table."

"I wouldn't vote for her anyway," Casey declared. "I don't want anybody telling me I can't have a shot of whiskey if I want it . . . man or woman. She'll be singing hymns from the bench."

Locke abruptly changed the subject. "Casey, have you ever tried a murder case?"

The tone of Locke's voice told Casey that the question was not a casual one.

"Yes."

"Could you tell me about one or two?"

This definitely was not an idle question. "Well, one case involved a Negro who was charged with murder after cutting off the private parts of a white man who had raped his wife. The man bled to death. The rape itself was nearly public. The man had dragged the woman into a livery stable and raped her in a horse stall while his drunken friends watched. A stable boy ran to summon the husband, and when he arrived, his rage was uncontrollable. He rendered justice right then and there. I spoke with some of the witnesses' wives about the importance of their husbands' testimony. The witnesses spoke the truth. The jury acquitted."

Locke said nothing and nodded for Casey to continue.

"The charges in the other case should never have been filed. Clearly self-defense. It took place at Rosa's, a bawdy house not far from the stockyards. A rancher, who had just sold his herd, decided to pay Rosa's a visit before heading back to the Sandhills. He took a notion to beat one of the prostitutes to a bloody pulp. She got free long enough to retrieve a Derringer she kept in a chamber pot and placed a bullet neatly between his eyes. It was an election year, and the Douglas County prosecutor was leading a crusade to rid Omaha of whores, so my client made a good target. I did a pretty fair job of keeping the good church folk off the jury, and we got an acquittal. The prosecutor, incidentally, lost the election after Rosa furnished *The Omaha Bee* with evidence that he had been one of her establishment's regular customers."

Locke said, "I have a murder case that might interest you."

"Yes, Ian," Emily jumped in with enthusiasm. "Casey would be perfect."

Casey's brow furrowed. "I don't understand. What are you talking about?"

"Just hear us out," Emily said. "Then you can make up your mind."

Over the next hour, Locke and Emily related the tangled story of Ralph Wainwright's murder. When they were finished, Emily looked at Casey expectantly. Locke was poker-faced. They had thrown her the bait and she knew she was hooked.

"I'm perplexed," Casey said. "It seems to me that the two of you have some interest in the conviction of Celeste Wainwright. She couldn't inherit under the holographic will then."

"But that wouldn't necessarily revive the earlier will," Locke said. The courts would likely rule that the estate would be distributed under the laws of intestacy, which would give the estate to Karl. Emily and I have agreed that the issues involving the wills should be determined on the merits. I want no involvement in the criminal aspects of the case. If criminal decisions become relevant, we will just let the chips fall where they may. If you take Celeste's case, I would not expect to discuss it further with you. We would need to maintain an impenetrable wall between our two cases."

"This is totally bizarre. Why, in heaven's name, would Celeste ask you to find her a lawyer?" She observed that Locke seemed a bit discomfited by her query. Interesting.

"I guess she trusts me. We've known each other for some time. We were . . . Close . . . at one time."

She noticed a faint blush on his cheeks. Of course. He'd slept with the woman. Well, at least, to his credit, it left him with a sense of obligation. It made no difference to Casey. "Can Celeste Wainwright, or whatever her name is, pay a reasonable fee?"

"She goes by Wainwright. Yes, I would think she could pay your fees. She's led me to believe she has modest assets of her own . . . including the Wainwright mansion. You would have to talk to her about that."

"Yes, but first she will have to decide if she wants to employ my services. She may not be all that delighted with the lawyer you've selected for her. She has to make the final decision."

"I take it you are interested in taking the case."

"Interested, yes. I'm willing to go to Borderview and talk to Mrs. Wainwright. At that time, we'll determine if we are a suitable attorney-client match. I'll see if I can catch a Friday train. That way I can stay the weekend, if necessary. Can you make arrangements for accommodations there?"

"I'll reserve a room at The Fremont. It's the best hotel in town."

Emily smiled. "I should warn you, Casey. It's the only hotel. But it's not terrible."

Casey did not hear Emily. Her eyes were fastened on Locke's. She had thought of him as a prospective psychological study, but as he returned her gaze with an annoying little smirk on his otherwise expressionless face, she wondered who was studying whom.

12

Ian

I LEANED BACK in my seat and tugged the brim of my hat down to ward off the sun from my eyes. I figured I might as well attempt a nap, since the conversation with my traveling companion had dead-ended a few minutes out of Omaha. We had another four hours of potential silence before the train pulled into Borderview, and the father-daughter reunion wasn't off to a very promising start. So far, Amanda Locke had not displayed a very impressive vocabulary. Since our departure from Omaha, her responses to my clumsy efforts at sparkling conversation had been confined pretty much to stony silences and an occasional "yes, sir' or "no, sir."

I glanced at Mandy who sat next to me in the window seat gazing at the vast prairie that rolled by as the train rocked and chugged its way along the endless ribbon of steel that sliced through the crazy quilt of rolling hills and grasslands and flat, fertile river bottoms that were southeast Nebraska, home to farmer, rancher and shopkeeper. I suspected that it all seemed lonely and desolate to a city girl, especially one who felt she had been abandoned by her mother and given up to a father who in some ways was a comparative stranger.

Still, we had shared a home once, and I had seen her weekly while I remained in Omaha, although never far from Nadine's watchful eye. After I made the move to Borderview, I had been nearly obsessed with efforts to be a part of her life, but her mother insisted Mandy wanted nothing to do with me, and I felt impotent to squeeze my way back into her life. I never quit, but I did come to accept that at best I could only hope time would grant opportunities to forge new bonds. When I was a boy, the Judge always said I had more persistence than brains—more often he called it stubbornness—but he assured me that my inclination to stick to a task would serve me well. I had never given up on Mandy, no matter what she thought, and I would stay the course with her whatever storms came our way.

Regardless, I did not desire to repeat the scene at the Omaha railroad station. Nadine had been a bit late, as was her habit, and had arrived with her coachman and Mandy in a buggy full of assorted bags about ten minutes before departure time. The conductor had not been pleased with the unexpected baggage, but saw to its loading while Mandy proceeded to throw a first class fit, screaming and sobbing and begging her mother not to leave her, insisting she would not go. Nadine, to her credit, remained firm in her resolve, and I could see the torment in her eyes when she told Mandy, "You have no choice in the matter, Amanda. I'm sorry. I love you more than life, but I have made this decision. You will go with your father. I will contact you when Victor and I return, and I will write every week."

She had given Mandy a desperate hug, and tears streamed down her cheeks as she whirled and rushed away to her waiting coach. I had done nothing that I knew of to create this unpleasant situation, but somehow at that moment I felt like the lowest kind of thief, and the angry glare I got from Mandy's cobalt blue eyes when the conductor chanted the last boarding call gave me no reason to feel otherwise.

I furtively studied my daughter's profile while she deliberately averted any look in my direction—she could not have been that mesmerized by the passing flora and fauna. Even discounting a father's pride, she would be a striking beauty someday. Her hair was the color of ripe wheat, and her skin, while fair, seemed to take well to the summer sun and assume more of an almond tint with the advance of the season. She had the long, gangly legs of a young colt, and she promised to be quite tall, as were most of the Lockes. But anyone who encountered her would most remember the haunting, penetrating eyes, the same eyes that had delivered her wrathful message before we boarded the train. With that thought I drifted into the first deep sleep I had experienced in days.

An hour or so later I was awakened abruptly by Mandy's voice. "It's okay for you to call me 'Mandy' if you want."

I pushed my hat back and straightened up in my seat, trying to reorient myself. I turned to my daughter, who was looking at me intently now, but without the earlier rancor.

"I know Mother doesn't like for you to call me 'Mandy,' but lots of my friends do, and I prefer it, actually."

"Good, then 'Mandy' it is." I decided to let her take the lead in our conversation, since my efforts at directing our dialogue had thus far been pretty much of a flop.

"Is it true we're going to live on a ranch?"

"I guess you'd call it a ranch, but it's a very small one."

"Do we sleep in a dugout?"

I smiled and shook my head. "No. There aren't but a few dugouts left in our part of the state. Our house is constructed mostly of native limestone. It's one-story, fairly small, but you'll have your own bedroom."

"Do you have a cook?"

"Just me. I have a good cook stove, but I'm not exactly famous for my culinary skills."

"Culinary?"

"A fancy word for cooking."

"I like words. How do you spell it?"

I spelled the word.

"Culinary. I always wanted to help the cook, but Mother would never allow me. Do you suppose I could learn some culinary skills at your house?"

"Of course. And if I can't teach you enough, we'll find someone who can."

For the first time there was a glint of enthusiasm in her eyes. "Can I ride your horses? I'm a good rider. I love horses."

"I'll borrow or buy a mare from my friend, George Washington. My gelding, Hemlock, is a little headstrong. My other two horses are broke for the buggy and aren't that good for riding."

"George Washington. Hemlock. Those are strange names."

"Hemlock's a kind of poison. Hemlock's a handsome Appaloosa, but he's always had a nasty temperament, even as a colt, and somehow I just thought the name suited him. George Washington is a neighbor and my best friend. I'll tell you more about him later. He's got a daughter your age . . . Rosemary. I think the two of you might hit it off."

Her mood darkened again, and she spoke in a near whisper.

"I have lots of friends in Omaha."

I was silent for some moments before I replied. "Mandy, I understand that you don't want to go to Borderview, but your mother decided it was best, and I know she has good reasons. I could see that it broke her heart to let you go. Selfishly, I'm darn glad you came with me. We haven't seen much of each other, and I want to know you, and I want you to know me. Nobody could love you more than I do, and I'll take care of you. I hope you'll come to think of this as a great adventure, and that eventually, no matter how long you stay, my home will always be your home."

Tears began to roll down her cheeks, and suddenly she clutched me tightly and pressed her head against my chest. She began to sob softly, and I put my arms around her and held her closely while she let out her pain. This young lady was hurting, and it wasn't just the ordeal of visiting her father. The reasons for Nadine's sudden change of heart about my suitability as a parent were shrouded with mystery, but I could see no point in trying to search out the story. In due time I would know if Nadine's motives were important. For the first time in years I felt like a father again, and I was damned well going to savor this moment.

13

Ian

GEORGE WASHINGTON AND his daughter, Rosemary, were waiting when Mandy and I stepped off the passenger car. George shook my hand with his iron grip and grinned broadly, his store-bought teeth gleaming like pearls against mahogany skin. "Welcome home, friend. Who's the pretty lady?"

"George, this is my daughter, Mandy, as if you didn't already know. And, Mandy, these are my neighbors, George Washington and Rosemary. I told you George had a daughter your age, but I didn't expect you'd meet her this soon."

Rosemary smiled shyly, her dark eyes friendly but uncertain.

"Hi," Mandy said, "my dad said you love horses, too."

Rosemary nodded agreement, and Mandy stepped forward and took her hand and led her away from the clueless fathers. In a matter of moments, the eleven-year-olds were engaged in animated girl talk of some kind.

George chuckled in amusement as we gathered up the bags. "That little gal of yours doesn't know strangers, does she? Rosemary was scared to come with me. She's so timid, I was afraid I'd have a helluva time getting her to talk, but Mandy didn't take any time at all drawing her out. I surely hope they continue to get on with each other. Rosemary just don't make friends easy—spends too much time alone. Mandy could be good for her."

"Hopefully, they'll be good for each other, but only time will tell. You and I won't have any more to say about their friendship. In the end it's up to them."

I followed George to the buckboard he'd driven into town and saw that Hemlock was tethered to the rear, TJ was dozing in the wagon bed. "How'd you know when I'd be in and that Rosemary's presence would be welcome?"

The stocky Pawnee tossed the bags on the wagon and lifted the girls up to the wagon bed just as effortlessly. George's strength was legend, and the flannel shirt could not hide the muscles that rippled in his arms and shoulders. The coal-black hair that dropped a bit over the ears and covered the back of his neck further belied a man who had recently eased past his sixtieth birthday. "I was in your office this morning to sign the papers for the McDowell land, and Will told me he'd got a telegram that you were coming back this afternoon and you were bringing company with you. I told him I'd pick you up at the station. God knows you work that man like a slave and he doesn't need to be your coachman, too."

"Well, I'm obliged. Things have happened so fast, I haven't had time to make any arrangements or figure out how I'm going to handle my new responsibilities, welcome as they are."

The girls continued to chatter like a couple of magpies, and TJ nestled into Mandy's lap as George and I climbed into the wagon seat, and he headed his team down the road.

"I've presumed to make a few arrangements on your behalf,"

George said. "Subject to your approval, of course. Martha sent some fresh-baked bread over to your place with me. And some smoked ham with pinto beans . . . and a cherry cobbler. Mandy needs to start off with a decent meal. They may be few and far between if you're doing the cooking. Tomorrow, you bring her back into town and show her around . . . treat her to lunch at Reuben's. Rosemary and I will come by your office early afternoon and take her out to our place till you see fit to show up again. She can spend a lot of time at our teepee if she wants."

George's "teepee" was a massive two-story limestone structure that included wings for housing the families of his married children and their families, more dormitory than house. George did nothing in a small way.

"I don't have any better ideas at the moment, George. I don't know what I'd do without you to run my life. I do need one more favor. I've got to find a horse for Mandy."

"You'll see a strawberry roan mare in the corral when we get to your Lazy Key. She's gentle, but strong and fast. If your girl likes her, we can trade for the legal work you and Will did on the McDowell deal."

"Without even seeing the mare, I'll bet I'm getting the best of the trade."

"I want to keep my lawyer happy. I've got some plans that take more brains than I've got to carry out."

"Yeah, you're dumb like a damn fox."

"Well, I'm just smart enough to know when to hire men smarter than me from time to time."

I studied the sky. We should be home in half an hour, well before sundown. No signs of a storm cloud. The drought lingered. It promised to be a long summer in more ways than one. My thoughts drifted to my work. The law is too much of what I am, and I cannot ever quite escape it. "George," I said. "Anything I should know about the Wainwright case."

"Probably."

"I'm listening."

"You might want to talk to Greta Kleine. No, you ought to have Will talk to her."

"Why Will?"

"He's more her age. And he's kind of an innocent. He might be too kindhearted for his own good sometimes, but women sense his gentleness and tell him things they wouldn't confess to a priest. Greta would likely tell him some things you need to know. All due respect, Ian, you can be kind of intimidating to somebody who doesn't know you. Downright scary, sometimes."

I bristled a bit, but knew George spoke the truth on all counts. "You obviously have some information. Why not save me some time and tell me what you know?"

"I don't know anything, but my boys married into the German community, and one of the women heard something. That's all I'll say. Damn it, Ian, I ain't going to do all of your work for you."

"I'll put Will on it in the morning. Thanks. Anything else I should know?"

"Ralph's son has been hanging around Borderview better than two weeks. Don't know why, but he's been bunking in the old line shack in Coyote Canyon. I bought the canyon pasture from Ralph a few years back. Karl probably doesn't know his old man sold the place. Anyway, I saw smoke when I rode out that way to check some first-calf heifers I'd put there, and there was an unsaddled horse outside the shack. I waited and watched a spell, and eventually old Karl popped out of the shack to take a piss. I left him be. Figured with a snake like him I'd just as soon know where he's sleeping."

"So he was in the county at least ten days before Ralph was killed?"

"By my count. I don't know how long he was here before I saw him."

"Did you tell Ike Bell about this?"

"He didn't ask."

George didn't have much use for Sheriff Ike Bell. And Ike Bell didn't have much use for Indians and didn't make any bones about it. He worked overtime trying to catch George stepping on the wrong side of the law and resented my Pawnee friend's success in what Ike thought should be the white man's world.

I wanted to pump George for some more information, but the wagon pulled to a stop at the gate of the Lazy Key. Mandy stopped her chatter and came to the front of the wagon. "What's that mean?" she asked, pointing to the sign on the gate.

"That's supposed to be the outline of a key lying on its back. It's our brand. The Lazy Key. That's what I call this little spread."

Her eyes lit with understanding, and she wrinkled her nose in a grin. "Oh, I get it. Key. Locke." She rested her hand on my shoulder. "It doesn't make that much sense, but I guess it doesn't matter what you call it, as long as it's home."

"Yes, Princess, it's home."

14

Ian

I SAT AT my desk thumbing through some hornbooks in search of any obscure principle of law that might support the contention that I should be appointed special administrator for Ralph's estate. Statehood had come to Nebraska less than twenty years earlier, and there was no significant body of State Supreme Court precedent yet upon which lawyers could rely. Thus, a decision rendered by a Massachusetts court some hundred years ago might be persuasive to a Nebraska judge, although it was doubtful Judge Helvey would give undue weight to the opinions of some judge he had never heard of and whose highfalutin words were beyond understanding. On the other hand, Reuben carried more common sense into a courtroom than most Harvard-educated lawyers. I hasten to add that I am a Yale man myself.

It was past closing time Monday, more than a week now since Ralph met his maker. The hearing on our petition for my appointment as special administrator was set for ten o'clock the next morning, and I had elected to stay over at the Fremont this night. Mandy and TJ were sleeping over at George's, to hers and

Rosemary's mutual delight. They had become inseparable in the few days since Mandy's arrival in Cottonwood County, and TJ had been sticking to Mandy like glue, treating me with some disdain unless it was feeding time. I had been pleasantly surprised, though, to find Mandy adapting quickly to the flow of life here. In some ways, this seemingly smooth transition baffled and worried me. It was inconsistent with the drama that had unfolded at the Omaha railroad station, and I had a sense that things were not quite as they appeared to be. My brother, Cam, though, always chides me for borrowing trouble and says I spend too much time looking for something to worry about. I reply, "Expect the worst; then you won't be disappointed." I have to work at being optimistic and have to plan to be spontaneous.

Anyway, the unexpected domestic tranquility was welcome, as events had been unfolding rapidly since my return to Borderview. Casey McGlaun had arrived Friday, had met at some length with Celeste at the county jail, spoke Saturday morning with Jess Cooper, the young County Attorney, and then left on the afternoon train. I found myself disappointed at not seeing her, but I appreciated it was best that I step back from the criminal case in light of my conflict with the accused in the probate dispute. Of course, the small town network via a visit by Will to the courthouse this morning had satisfied my curiosity about the essentials. Indeed, Celeste had employed Casey to represent her. In fact, she had signed a mortgage of the Wainwright house in favor of Casey to secure payment of the lawyer's fees. Albert Sweeney had filed the document with the register of deeds when the courthouse opened this morning, and this pleased me immeasurably, for I am certain he was greatly insulted by Celeste's employment of other counsel to handle the criminal case. And it had to gall him yet more that Casey had a first lien against the property for her fees. I had yet to witness Casey's skills as an advocate, but I was impressed by her aggressiveness as a businesswoman.

With no particular authority to do so, and hoping Judge Helvey would make me an honest man, I had contracted Cash Berry's services for a funeral of sorts for Ralph at the Methodist Church this Wednesday. Ralph wasn't a Roman Catholic or Episcopalian, the only other representatives of Christian grace in Borderview, and the Methodists were generous about claiming anybody else who needed a church home for baptism, marriage or funeral, whether duly enrolled or not. Although I confined my own church attendance to funerals and an occasional wedding, the good Methodist pastor considered me more or less an honorary member of his congregation based upon my brother Franklin's clerical credentials in the denomination.

Reverend Tobias Hill would preside over an empty coffin at the service, because Casey McGlaun had instructed in no uncertain terms to Jess Cooper that Ralph's body was not to be disturbed further until a physician she would send from Omaha completed an examination of the remains. Cash Berry had observed that the body could not have been brought into the church in any event, because the stench would have sickened the congregation. Cash was still disgruntled about the turn of events that had deprived him of a first class funeral. It had been necessary for me to personally guarantee payment of the funeral bill in light of the uncertain disposition of the banker's estate. I confess that I do not share Casey McGlaun's business acumen.

I had just come across an obscure Ohio court decision on point when I heard the door of the outer office open. I assumed that Will had returned from his attempt to interview Greta Kleine, and anticipation of his report was no small part of my motive for remaining in the office late. Two soft taps on my door confirmed my assumption.

"Come on in, Will," I called without getting up.

Will entered my office, nodded, and let himself down slowly into the chair nearest my desk. His face was grim, devoid of its usual boyish innocence, and he slumped like a bag of rags in the chair. Will Heasty had aged noticeably this day.

"You look bushed," I said, stating the obvious.

Will took a deep breath and sighed. "I am much happier at my typewriter. I don't know if I'm cut out for the people part of this business."

"Greta was a tough interview I gather."

"Once we broke the ice, she was more than cooperative. She wouldn't stop talking. It's what she had to say that boggles my scrambled brain. She left me with a terrible load on my mind. But you're the boss, so I'll let you sort it out."

"Did she know something about the holographic will?"

"Not specifically. But she said Albert Sweeney had been calling at the Wainwright house for several months before Ralph's death."

"To visit Ralph?"

"No. To visit Celeste. And, according to Greta, the visits had a . . . a social side."

"Celeste was sleeping with Albert?"

"So it appears. Tuesdays and Thursdays. Regular as clockwork. After Ralph left for the bank in the morning, Albert showed up to spend an hour or so in the master bedroom with Celeste. Afterward they would go in the library and huddle over papers Celeste had removed from Ralph's desk. Strangely, neither seemed to be bothered by Greta's presence in the house. Their liaisons were quite rambunctious and noisy, according to Greta." At this remark, Will's face turned tomato red. "Can you imagine talking about such things with a young woman . . . one you've never met before?"

I could not imagine Will talking about such things with any young woman. Regardless, George's appraisal of Greta's listening skills had been on target. I shook my head in disbelief. "Celeste and Albert. I never would have thought." I was not only shocked; I was halfway insulted. I had expected Celeste to have better taste. This was an ill reflection on her other lovers, myself included. My fantasies turned to ashes then and there. Remembrances of my past with Celeste would never be the same.

Will said, "Celeste and Ralph hadn't shared a bedroom for a year or more. Ralph slept in one of the guest rooms."

"Well, obviously, Albert had the opportunity to coach Celeste on the finer points of making a holographic will. This also explains why he was named executor of the holographic. Did Greta know anything about Ralph's signing a new will?"

"Not specifically. But she lived in the maid's quarters six days out of seven and saw everything that went on in the house. About a week before Ralph was killed, she heard Ralph and Celeste having a dogfight in the library. It had something to do with signing some papers or writing a letter. Greta heard Celeste scream at Ralph 'sign it or I'll send for Ike Bell right now.'"

"She could have been referring to the will, but that's pretty much speculation at this juncture."

"Celeste had another visitor."

"A lover?"

"It appears not. Karl Wainwright. He came around while Ralph was at work, too, on at least two occasions during the week before Ralph's death. He and Celeste were very secretive and took great care to close the door to the library and speak softly when they met."

"Did Greta say if Ralph knew Karl was in town?"

"He knew. Greta told him."

Something in Will's voice caught my attention. "Greta told Ralph about Karl? What about Albert?"

"Him, too. Ralph was reasonably well informed about what was going on in the home . . . thanks to Greta."

"You haven't told me everything."

Will pulled a handkerchief from his jacket and dabbed at his brow. There was a welcome cool breeze drifting in the office window, and it was not the condition of the room that was the source of his perspiration. "This is unbelievably complicated, Ian. You see, Greta was, euphemistically speaking, sleeping with Ralph."

"Oh, shit. This cannot be happening. You've made this all up to drive me nuts." It was enough to drive a vital man to celibacy.

Will shrugged, seemingly at a loss for words.. "This is what she told me."

"Do you believe her?"

"I believe her."

"And how long, euphemistically speaking, had Ralph and Greta been sleeping together?"

"Something less than a year. At first Ralph visited the maid's quarters just to talk, and then one thing led to another, you know."

"I know." How well I knew.

"Anyway, Celeste gave them ample opportunity to be together with her famed shopping expeditions to Lincoln and Omaha, and all. When Celeste was absent, Greta shared Ralph's upstairs bedroom, and he, needless to say, spent less time at the bank . . . until Celeste came home a day early a few months back."

"And she caught them doing the dirty deed?"

"Yep. Opened the bedroom door and found the two of them naked as jaybirds. Greta was humiliated."

"But she was still working in the house after Ralph's death. I saw her there."

"Oh yes. Celeste never said a word when she saw them there. Just turned around and left the room. Later, Greta was packing her clothes in anticipation of a move, and Celeste walks in and tells her to get started on the laundry. Just like nothing ever happened. A week later, Ralph comes calling at the maid quarters and things are just like they were before . . . only Ralph says they can't ever use the upstairs bedroom again. He claimed he had told Celeste he planned to marry Greta, but that he would make it right with Celeste financially if she just let things go on the way they were for a spell."

"Did Greta know Ralph and Celeste weren't actually married?"

"No. And I didn't tell her otherwise. Didn't think it was my place." Will hesitated. "There's something else."

I didn't like the way he said that. "Yes."

"Greta's carrying a child."

I leaned back, and my eyes bore in on Will until he fidgeted in his chair. "Is this the end of your surprises?"

"Uh, yes, I think so. Yes."

"And the child is Ralph's?"

"Well I believe it is. That is, I believe Greta. She doesn't seem like the sort that would sleep with more than one man at a time . . . I mean—"

"I know what you mean. On the other hand, she was willing to sleep with an apparently married man while his apparent wife slumbered one floor above the conjugal bed."

"I know how it looks. But she says she loved Ralph and that he was her first and only. All I can say is what I said before . . . I believe what she told me."

I felt a bit callous, putting Will on the defensive like that. He had done a magnificent piece of investigative work, although I was uncertain how his information impacted either the murder charges or our probate case. "Has she talked to anyone else about this?"

"She says not . . . other than her parents."

"Not even Ike Bell? She would obviously have been a potential witness."

"No, Ike never talked to her."

So much for Sheriff Bell's investigative skills. Ike wouldn't recognize evidence if he stepped on it. But a witness had come forward, and surprisingly the name hadn't leaked from the courthouse yet.

"Did you explain to Greta that your conversation with her wasn't necessarily confidential . . . that we might have to pass anything you learned onto the authorities?"

"Yes, I think she just wanted somebody to listen to her without judging her. And I would never do that, being just another sinner myself. I guess her folks are raising all kinds of hell, old Gerhardt especially. Says she's disgraced the family name. She won't tell them who the father is, but they've got it figured out. And, of course, there's no man to shotgun into marriage."

"What are her plans for the baby?"

"She'll have to give it up for adoption. The child would be a constant reminder of her shame, she says. She doesn't have the means to support herself and a child, too. Besides, she doesn't want the baby to start life with the stigma of 'Greta's bastard.'"

"I think we can help her. Emily Stanton's on the board of trustees of the Omaha Children's Home. They maintain a home for unwed mothers, and Greta could go there to live until she has the baby. If she still wants to give the baby up for adoption at that time, they'll help with arrangements. Either way, the people at the home will help her find work if she doesn't want to come back here. She can get legal advice there, too. I don't think an illegitimate child has any legal claim to Ralph's estate under Nebraska law, and parentage is virtually impossible to establish in the courts. Still, Ralph's apparently left behind some moral responsibilities for somebody to clean up, and, if Emily ends up with the estate, I'd bet she'll want to look after Greta and the baby."

Will brightened noticeably. "I'd really feel better if we could help her, Ian."

"Emily's coming in for Ralph's funeral. I'll talk to her about it. Perhaps, we can arrange for her to meet Greta while she's here." Apparently, the firm of Locke & Heasty would be practicing law with a bit of social conscience. Will's innate decency could be contagious.

"Now," I said, "to keep our noses clean, we need to inform

the law of anything we've learned that might be pertinent to the criminal prosecution. I don't trust Ike Bell's mouth with this information. I suggest you have a chat with Jess Cooper tomorrow and tell him the gist of what you've told me. A quick summary will do. We have an obligation to disclose, but we don't have to do all their work for them. Ask Jess to be discreet for the sake of the young woman. He's a good man, and he won't go beyond the facts necessary to make his case. Greta's probably going to have to testify, though, and that makes it all the more important we make arrangements for her to leave here when the trial's over. A lot of our good Christian folk aren't as kind and forgiving as you, Will."

"What does this do to our case?"

"I'd say you've turned over a few rocks, and now we have to look under them and start digging. All we really have, though, are suspicions, and that's not enough for tomorrow's hearing."

15

Ian

THE COTTONWOOD COUNTY courtroom was a box that would hold no more than a dozen occupants, including judge and counsel, comfortably. The judge's bench was a small wooden table set on the same level as the other Spartan furniture, and it was framed by a large window that furnished tolerable light on a sunny day like this one. Two counsel tables, each with several chairs for lawyers and their clients, were positioned perpendicular to the judge's bench, so the lawyers might face each other and exchange glares of contempt or disdain when occasion called for it. Three or four chairs behind each counsel table constituted a gallery for spectators or functioned as a jury box when a six-man county court jury was impaneled. The space was generally adequate for the probates, guardianships, misdemeanors and small civil lawsuits under the jurisdiction of the county court, which rarely offered the kind of carnival that drew a crowd.

I arrived early, as was my habit. Furthermore, counsel tables were claimed on the basis of first appearance and I had a distinct preference for the table to the judge's right. It was an irrational predilection, much like the churchgoer who sits in the same pew each Sunday, but I just was not as comfortable at the other table.

I dropped my tattered, leather briefcase on the table and thereby staked my claim. The briefcase had been a gift from my father upon my admission to the Nebraska bar, and, although it had more than served its time, I could not yet abandon it for the new, sleeker model that had sat in my office closet these past five years. I felt I was more open to new ideas and ways of doing things than most of those in a tradition-bound profession, but certain things gave me a sense of continuity and constancy in my life, and my briefcase was foremost among those.

I pulled back a chair and sat down. I picked a few of TJ's hairs from my black coat and then opened the briefcase and spread its contents on the table. My coat would confine me in a hotbox this morning, but coat and tie were a lawyer's uniform and mandated by most judges as a symbol of respect. I glanced out the window behind the judge's table and waved at two boys who stood on the boardwalk outside with their noses pressed to the glass. On a summer day, there were often more observers outside the window than in the courtroom itself.

Momentarily, the courtroom door creaked open and Albert Sweeney stepped in, dapper and stylish in his blue pinstripe suit, his thinning black hair slicked back and his pencil-thin mustache properly waxed. No cat hairs on Prince Albert's coat, I noted. No, Albert was nothing if not fastidious. Even though he was slightly overweight and had a pregnant paunch, his wardrobe was tailored carefully to cover any unseemly bulges. I wondered what Celeste had thought when she got her first glimpse of Albert's naked body. Disappointment and dismay, I hoped. Probably had a grub worm for a pecker.

Sweeney smiled broadly when he saw me. "Good morning,

counselor," he said as he placed his polished, black briefcase on the vacant table. He plucked a gold watch from his vest pocket and examined it. "Early as usual, I see."

"Morning, Albert," I replied. Morning, asshole, I thought. I enjoyed a congenial relationship with most members of the county bar, but I could not suffer Sweeney and admitted I had no objectivity where the man was concerned.

"Ian, I wondered if we might have a word before the judge takes the bench. I have a proposal for your consideration, and we might be able to resolve this by stipulation."

"I'm listening."

"It seems to me that since I'm designated executor in Ralph's most recent will, the judge is very likely to appoint me as special administrator for the estate. Your chances of prevailing in probate of the earlier will are less than slim. Nonetheless, my client would like to settle any dispute as amicably as possible. We are prepared to enter into an agreement whereby Miss Stanton would receive distribution of twenty per cent of the estate, in consideration for which you and she would dismiss the petition for probate of the earlier will and consent to my appointment as special administrator pending probate of the holographic will."

"Are you serious, Albert?"

"Very serious. This is your client's final opportunity to get something from the estate. She'd be a fool not to grab it. I understand she will arrive on the afternoon train. If you wish to speak to her about this offer, I would be willing to stipulate to a continuance of this hearing for a few days. I'm certain the judge would be pleased to have the parties settle this case."

I leaned forward on the counsel table and studied my adversary. The man was not just bluster. He believed his own words. When Albert Sweeney accepted a case, he became a true believer. His client could do no wrong. Sweeney carried the banner for truth and justice. This supreme confidence in the rightness of the cause encouraged clients to pursue cases beyond good sense and lose needless dollars in the process. Furthermore, Sweeney tended to be blind to chinks in his own case, and, as a result, he was frequently poorly prepared for the opposing lawyer's assault on his evidence and theory of the case. Still, the guy could be slick, and he could charm the unwary often enough to make a decent living.

"I don't need to speak with Miss Stanton. I have total authority to make any decision."

Sweeney smiled. "That's wonderful. Have we struck a bargain then?"

I shook my head in disbelief and did not bother to reply. I commenced shuffling through my notes, while Sweeney waited expectantly for a response. Moments later two spectators entered the room and took seats. I recognized one of the observers as a clerk from the county treasurer's office, probably anointed as the courthouse crier to carry embellished news of the proceedings back to his superior. The other man was vaguely familiar, but I could not place him. He was a diminutive man in his thirties, with flaxen hair and a sparse moustache that barely formed a shadow on a colorless face. His pale blue eyes seemed emotionless. Sweeney turned and saw the man and acknowledged his presence with a nod and a smile. It suddenly occurred to me that this had to be Karl Wainwright. His straight, narrow nose and dimpled chin were descended from Ralph.

Abruptly, the door opened again, and the Honorable Reuben Helvey entered the room. The lawyers arose in unison from their chairs, and the spectators took the cue and followed suit. The black-robed judge looked very much his part as he made his way to his table-bench. A burley, ruddy-faced man with thick white hair, Judge Helvey might have been a formidable figure were it not for the dark eyes that darted nervously from one lawyer to the other and betrayed his lack of confidence.

"Be seated," the judge announced in a high-pitched voice that did not quite fit his appearance. The judge thumbed through the folders on his desk, while the lawyers waited for some direction. After an appropriate period of silence, he looked up and sighed heavily. He looked first at Sweeney and then at me. "I don't suppose you boys have worked something out between you."

I responded, "No, your Honor, there's been no stipulation."

Sweeney stood and said, "Your Honor, on behalf of Mrs. Wainwright, I have made a generous settlement offer to Mr. Locke, and I want you to be aware that we have made every effort to save the court the trouble and unnecessary inconvenience of a hearing in this matter."

"Sit down, Albert. I get paid for listening to you law wranglers, and if we need a hearing, that's what we'll have." The judge looked down at the papers in his file folder and tugged at his ear before he spoke. "Now let's just be sure we're all riding in the same wagon this morning. This is my understanding of what we're here for. There have been two wills filed for probate. One will was signed, witnessed and dated May 10, 1883 and filed for probate by Ian. This will names Ian as executor. There is another will allegedly written by Ralph Wainwright in his own hand and dated June 1, 1884. This will appoints Albert as executor. A probate hearing on both of these said wills is set for August 16 and cannot be held before that date because required legal notices must be given and the statutory waiting periods must expire."

The judge looked at the lawyers over his wire-rimmed bifocals. "Any arguments so far?"

"None, your Honor," I said.

Sweeney arose from his chair. "Your Honor, I would just call to your attention that our will and petition were filed first."

"Sit down, Albert. You'll have plenty of chances to speak your piece. I just want to make it clear what we're taking up this morning." The judge continued. "Now we all know that I'm not going to rule on either will until the charges against Mrs. Wainwright or Miss Kimball, or whatever her name is, are settled one way or another. So we all know the August 16 hearing probably isn't really going to happen on August 16 and that only God knows when that hearing is going to take place. Now, our problem is that Ralph left bills to pay and businesses to run, including Wainwright Savings Bank where I've got my meager funds that I'd like somebody looking after. So somebody's got to run the show until this convoluted mess gets cleaned up. And that's what the special administrator does. When a will is admitted to probate and an executor's appointed, the special administrator will file his accounting with this court and hit the road. Both of you gentlemen want that job, so it seems to me I got three choices. I can appoint Ian. I can appoint Albert. Or I can appoint anybody I else I damn well please." The judge looked at the lawyers again. "Are you still with me, gentlemen?"

I nodded in the affirmative. Actually, Reuben, uncomfortable as he was with the dilemma, understood his task well and had set the stage very succinctly.

Sweeney got up again. "May it please the court—"

"It don't please the court, Albert. Do you agree with what I said or not?"

"Well, as far as it goes, but I would like—"

"That's as far as it goes, Albert, so I'd say it's time to get this wagon rolling. Since you made the fuss about filing your petition first, we'll just let you be first out of the chute. You just start things off and tell me why I ought to put you in charge of Ralph's estate."

Sweeney was impervious to insult, and he was unflappable in a courtroom. Nothing he said embarrassed him because the moment words spilled from his mouth they became truth according to the Book of Sweeney. It never occurred to him that others, on occasion, might see him as a pompous fool. Once again, he arose and cleared his throat and looked around the court at some invisible crowd gathered there. "May it please the court, I wish to congratulate your Honor on your learned and excellent summation of this case. I hope I may submit our position with only a fraction of such eloquence."

Judge Helvey and I rolled our eyes simultaneously.

"Your Honor, this is a very serious matter we have before the court, and I know from your splendid record on the bench you fully appreciate the importance of the decision you are being forced to make. Ralph Wainwright was a giant in our community, respected as citizen and businessman. His passing leaves a void that will probably never be filled. Yet, those who are left behind must forge ahead. As you know, Mr. Wainwright was an entrepreneur with wide-ranging and complex business interests that must be inventoried and managed during this most critical period. Not the least of these interests is Wainwright

Savings Bank. Protection of the estate's assets is of utmost urgency not only to Mr. Wainwright's presumptive devisees, but to all of Cottonwood County, for the failure of the bank would be the fall of the first domino in a long line. The person who is appointed special administrator of this estate will have an awesome responsibility and must be a man of spotless integrity and must possess no small amount of business acumen. Your appointee will be acting in a fiduciary capacity for heirs and community—"

The judge interrupted. "Albert, if it will help move things along, I assure you this is a decision I take seriously . . . as I do all of my decisions."

"I would never suggest otherwise, your Honor. You have an enviable reputation among bar and community for your seriousness."

A look of exasperation crossed the judge's face. "Albert, just tell me why I should appoint you special administrator?"

"In the interest of time, your Honor, I will get right to the point."

"An excellent idea."

"First, your Honor, I should be granted priority to appointment because I am designated executor of the last will signed by the deceased prior to his death. Yes, I appreciate that this will is not destined to go unchallenged, but based upon all we now know, it is, indeed, the last will, and in the end I expect to be executor of it. In light of the probabilities, it makes good sense, for the sake of continuity that I be appointed to administer the estate during this unfortunate period when the estate is held hostage by frivolous legal antics."

My eyes bore in on Sweeney, but with no small effort I

maintained my silence. Let the bastard hang himself.

Sweeney continued. "Secondly, I am without doubt the more qualified of the applicants for this position. Although Mr. Locke and I are contemporaries, in a manner of speaking, I have been practicing law in this county for more than fifteen years, while Mr. Locke is a relative newcomer. I know this community and am attuned to its heartbeat. The community's interests will come first under my management of the estate, and I will administer the assets for the benefit of all. Furthermore, I am very experienced in the world of commerce, having represented many businessmen and farmers during my years of practice. I have served as executor of many estates, most of which have been under the watchful and competent eyes of this court. As for integrity, my reputation speaks for itself."

"Do you have any more to say, Albert?" the judge interjected.

Sweeney looked surprised at the question, apparently having much more to say. "Well, there is much more I could say. But if I may reserve rebuttal time, I will defer to Mr. Locke."

"Rebuttal reserved." The judge turned to me. "Ian, what you got to say for yourself?"

I stood and picked up some typed sheets of paper from the tabletop. "Judge, may I approach the bench?"

"Drop the formalities, Ian. Just give me what you got."

I placed the papers in front of the judge. "Judge, I'm submitting affidavits which have been signed by Cash Berry and Will Heasty as witnesses to the will dated May 10, 1883. The witnesses verify that Ralph signed the will in their presence, declared the document to be his last will and testament and requested that Cash and Will sign as witnesses. The affidavits also state that the witnesses signed in the presence of the testator and of each other. The will accordingly satisfies the statutory requirements for execution under Nebraska statutes."

"Objection, your Honor. This is not an evidentiary hearing on probate of the will. This is irrelevant to the issues before the court."

Judge Helvey tugged nervously at his ear. He preferred to avoid technical rulings wherever possible. "Ian, what do you say to that?"

"I'll explain the relevance, Judge. The will cannot be admitted to probate at this hearing, but Albert has already put the relative merits of the wills at issue by his contentions regarding the supposed superiority of the holographic will. He made the validity of the earlier will relevant if it had not been previously. I'm now entitled to address Albert's claims."

"Makes sense to me," the judge said. "Go ahead."

I handed the judge another sheet. "I've listed here court citations pertinent to this case and the principles of law that the cases represent. You will find several Nebraska cases that declare that a will that satisfies all of the statutory requirements of execution is presumed valid unless evidence is produced as to undue influence, duress, incompetence or some other fact going to the state of mind of the testator. In short, there can be little doubt that the 1883 will was valid. The issue ultimately will be whether it was subsequently revoked. That, of course, depends upon the validity of the alleged holographic will for which Albert has offered no proof. The court cases all indicate that a holographic will must satisfy a higher standard of proof."

"Objection," howled Sweeney.

"What's your basis, Albert?" the judge asked.

Sweeney was temporarily speechless. "This is unfair," he

stammered. "Opposing counsel did not have the courtesy to warn me he was going to raise evidentiary matters."

I declined to engage in a verbal duel with the other lawyer, confident the judge would recognize I had no obligation to do Sweeney's work for him.

Judge Helvey asked, "Anything else, Ian?"

"Addressing the issue of qualifications, Judge, I have a few comments. I would make it known to the court that I have a history of representing Ralph Wainwright regarding most of his business matters over the past five years. I have been serving as legal counsel for the bank, although I must tell you that Ralph was very secretive about his business dealings, and I am not intimately familiar with all of his commercial enterprises. I have the advantage of knowing where to find most of the answers, however. I would also inform the court that during the years I practiced in Omaha, I served as general counsel for the state's largest bank. Real estate and banking law were my areas of expertise. I submit that notwithstanding my being a relative newcomer to the community, my past experience would serve me well as special administrator. Whether my reputation for honesty rises to the level required of a fiduciary, I leave to the court." I returned to my seat.

The judge cocked his head and looked at Sweeney. "Albert, I said you could have rebuttal time, but I need to get over to the tavern to help with the lunch crowd. I'd take it kindly if you just called it good."

Put that way, Sweeney was trapped, and even he realized it. "I will waive rebuttal and rely upon the court's sense of justice to make a fair decision in this matter."

"Thank you, Albert. Gentlemen, I don't see any reason to

waste more time taking this under advisement. I'm appointing Ian Locke special administrator. No bond required. Ian, have Will fix up an order and letters of administration and I'll get them signed this afternoon. Good morning, Gentlemen."

16

Ian

IN THIS LIFE there are moments no amount of money can buy, and on this Saturday night, during that magic hour before sundown, I was savoring one of them. Mandy and I sat in two sturdy rocking chairs on the veranda, Mandy lost in the world of Louisa May Alcott's *Little Women*, and I, with my feet propped on the cedar porch rail, gazing dreamily at the undulating hills that rolled into Kansas some five miles to the south. A gentle breeze drifted in and coaxed us to remain for as long as we cared. We bathed in the serenity of silence. Later the nighttime choir would perform, coyotes mournfully howling in the distance, crickets chirping, bullfrogs croaking and owls hooting as their feathered relatives chimed in. But the music would be soft and soothing, as fireflies danced in before our eyes. I always knew peace at this place. Tonight, with my precious daughter beside me, I knew heaven.

It had been an eventful week. There had been the confrontation with Albert Sweeney in Reuben's courtroom, followed by Ralph's funeral on Wednesday. The county had turned out for the funeral, filling the church to overflowing, probably as much because of curiosity as for respect for the recently departed. The murder of a prominent banker would become a thing of legend in a rural county, and one's attendance at the funeral could fashion a tale for grandchildren. The empty coffin would add a bit of drama to the story. At least I now had authority to pay Ralph's funeral bill. An Omaha physician was to have examined the remains this morning, after which Cash would proceed with unceremonious burial. Graveside services were out of the question given the stench emanating from the fragmented corpse, and Cash and I agreed we did not want more fodder for the gossips.

I had spoken with Emily following Ralph's funeral. When I explained Greta's dilemma, she immediately promised to make arrangements at The Omaha Children's Home. *The Bee* had consented to her returning to Borderview to report on the trial in spite of her peripheral relationship to the story, and she would be back in a few weeks to do some background work. In fact, she expected to do a first person feature on her uncle and her remembrances of him. She would need to walk a fine line to maintain her credibility with the reader, but she was excited about giving it a try. In any case, while Emily was in town, she and Will would meet with Greta and work out the details for the young woman's move to Omaha immediately following the trial.

Emily also informed me that Casey McGlaun was working feverishly to put her Omaha caseload in order, so she could come to Borderview as soon as possible to begin trial preparation. The district judge expected to be in Borderview in a month or so to preside over Celeste's trial, and Casey planned to conduct her own exhaustive investigation. Somehow the idea of Casey coming to Borderview for an extended stay pleased me.

The murder case was not my responsibility, however, and my focus for the moment was the temporary administration of Ralph's estate, which was proving to be no trivial task. I did not have a handle on the situation yet, but I smelled something rotten. Ralph had been unloading an exceptionally large amount of his personal investments in the weeks before his death, and no replacement assets showed up anywhere. I had reviewed the bank's note portfolio yesterday and found it sickly enough to cause me some worry. Much of my concern stemmed from the fact that Ralph ran a one-man operation at Wainwright Savings Bank. He was President and sole loan officer. The four other directors of the bank were farmers and merchants who served for the sole purpose of enhancing the public's confidence in the management. They were honest, respected men, but they knew nothing about the operation of a bank. They collected token directors' fees each month and basked in the prestige of their offices.

The basking might be coming to an end. I had called a special directors' meeting for Monday morning. As special administrator, I voted all of Ralph's bank shares. The shareholders elect the bank directors, and since Ralph owned all of the shares, he had the power to elect and remove directors at will. I would diplomatically inform the directors that they were going to elect me President of the Wainwright Savings Bank.. Thereafter, Will would be taking on a still larger burden of the workload at the office for a while.

I also employed an accountant from Lincoln to conduct an audit of the bank and to try to reconstruct the trail of Ralph's financial transactions. The bank's cashier, who with a teller constituted the bank's only employees, had informed me that

Ralph had not engaged an independent auditor for at least three years. This news did nothing for my peace of mind.

"Dad?" Mandy's voice brought me back from my reverie. I turned my head and saw she had put her book aside and had evidently been watching me for a spell.

"What is it, Princess?" I scooted my rocker around to face her.

"Are you a dreamer?"

"A dreamer? I suppose you could say that. Anyway, I spend a lot of time in my own head. I have a lot of good conversations with myself up there. Am I making any sense?" She grinned, and I must say she absolutely owns me when she smiles and crinkles her pixie nose the way she does.

"Mother always says I'm a dreamer just like my father." She grinned again. "I don't think she always meant it as a good thing, though."

"Well, I suppose it's not always a good thing. Sometimes I'm at a meeting, and I get tired of listening to people yammer, so I just slip into my own world for a spell. But then I don't hear what's going on . . . and I guess it's rude besides."

"Yeah, I do that all the time. Lots of times I'd rather just be by myself and think about things. I love Rosemary. She's my best friend anywhere, but sometimes I even have to get away from her for a while. If I don't get my dreaming time, I get crabby."

"Me, too."

"There's a lot of time to dream here . . . like sitting on the porch at night, or during the day when I'm riding Dancer."

"Dancer?"

"I named my horse today. I've thought hard about it. She's so graceful and careful on her feet, like a dancer, I decided the name fit."

"It's a good name. Something to live up to."

"Maybe Hemlock's living down to his name. Maybe you should have named him something else."

"Too late now. He is what he is."

"Could I ride him some time?

The thought startled me, and I did not like the picture that flashed in my mind. "I don't know. I can barely handle him myself. We'll see. No promises."

"I like it here, Dad. I thought I'd hate it, but I was wrong. I miss Mother, but I'm okay."

"I'm glad, because whatever happens when your Mother returns, I don't want us to ever be separated like we were again."

"Me, either. If I go back to Omaha, I'll come here and visit as much as I can. Spend summers here with you, maybe."

"That would be wonderful."

"I just wish Mother could come and live here."

"I don't think she'd like living in Borderview."

"Not just Borderview. Here. On the Lazy Key."

Our conversation was taking an unexpected turn. "That can't be, Princess. That time is past."

There was a compelling sadness in her face now and a huskiness in her voice. "I've been thinking about that all week. About you and Mother and me all being together."

"Your mother has a husband, Mandy."

"She could divorce him. Just like she did you. Then she could marry you again."

"It doesn't work that way, honey."

Her eyes clouded with sudden anger. "I hate Victor," she hissed. "He hits Mother and he—"

"He what?"

"Nothing." She brushed a tear from her eye and her teeth dug in her lower lip before she turned away and picked up her book. Conversation ended. Don't push. Give her room. And time. Patience.

After a respectable silence, I said, "Tomorrow's Sunday, and I'm not going anywhere near the office. What would you like to do?"

"Go to church."

"Church?"

"Yes, don't you ever go to church?"

"Not much." Not a huge fib, if funerals counted.

"Do you belong to a church?"

I evaded the question. "I was baptized a Methodist. My mother was a Quaker, and my father didn't belong to a church. There wasn't a meeting place for Friends where we lived at the time, so my mother took the children to the Methodist Church. My brother, Franklin, is a Methodist preacher." I added the last comment, thinking that might count for something.

"I'm a Presbyterian."

"I know. I was there when you were baptized. We don't have a Presbyterian Church in Borderview, but Methodists aren't too far from Presbyterians in the way they look at things." That was a guess on my part, for a student of theology I am not.

"Then we can go to the Methodist Church."

"Well, okay." What else could I say? I supposed a father had some responsibility to expose his child to religious influence, and I guessed it wouldn't hurt me all that much. I hoped this wouldn't become a habit, though.

"Grandma Sarah was a Quaker? What do Quakers do?"

"I truthfully don't know all that much about them. They call their worship services 'meetings,' and I don't think they have a preacher as such. Different members speak at the meetings. They emphasize doing good works over religious rituals. They've established schools for Indians, and many Quakers worked to help slaves escape to the North. Most oppose war, and many will not take up arms. They're generally a quiet people who try to live their lives according to the way they interpret the bible."

"I never knew Grandma Sarah, but Mother says my middle name, Kate, came from her middle name."

"Yes. Your mother got to choose your first name, and I got to pick the middle name. I didn't like the ring of 'Amanda Sarah,' but 'Amanda Kate' had a nice sound. And I wanted to give you something of your grandmother. She was a remarkable woman."

"And Cammie was named after your twin brother."

"Yes."

"I don't remember him . . . or Grandpa Locke or Aunt Hannah or Uncle Franklin. And there's Uncle Thad, too, isn't there?"

"Yes, your Uncle Thad's a veterinary surgeon. You weren't more than three years old the last time you saw them. They all came to Omaha when I still lived there."

"Does Uncle Cam look like you?"

"Most strangers can't tell us apart, but Cam always claims he's the handsome one. I say I'm the smart one, because I'm older . . . by about five minutes."

Mandy rolled her eyes, and traces of a grin returned to her lips. "I'd like to meet Uncle Cam."

"You will. I've already written Cam and told him we'll be making a visit to the Circle L in September when it's cooler and, hopefully, I'm not so swamped with legal work. You'll meet your Aunt Pilar, Cam's wife, and their three kids . . . your cousins. And, of course, your Grandpa Locke. I haven't seen them since last Christmas, although Cam and I write back and forth all the time."

We were interrupted by a long, high-pitched yowl from the direction of the barn. I got up and stepped off the veranda. Momentarily, the horses began whinnying, and then I saw TJ limping up from the barn. Mandy jumped up and ran out into the ranch yard to meet him and scooped him into her arms.

"Dad," she said, "TJ's hurt."

The commotion continued in the barn. "Take him to the house, Mandy. I'll look at him in a minute." I whirled and ran into the house, plucked my Winchester from the gun rack, pumped a cartridge into the chamber and headed toward the barn.

As I approached the barn, I saw movement behind the side corral, something racing toward the arroyo that angled into a wooded area some distance from the farmstead. My instinct was to give chase, but dusk was settling in, and Mandy was alone at the house. The horses had quieted now, and Hemlock stuck his head out of the barn door and ventured out into the corral, followed momentarily by Dancer and the team. No harm there. I checked out the barn, and as I expected, I found nothing. As I made my way back to the house, I faced the truth. The figure I had seen running from behind the corral had not been *something*. It had been the shadowy form of *someone*.

Mandy was cradling TJ like a baby in her arms when I entered the house, and he was not resisting the attention, purring loudly, as she gently rubbed behind his ears. He had clearly shifted loyalties to the new member of the household. I took a look at him and could not detect any broken bones but found his left hip painful to the touch.

"Will he be okay, Dad?"

"I think so. If he's crippled up in the morning, I'll ask George to take a look at him . . . after church, of course. We don't have a vet in town, but George is pretty good at doctoring sick or injured animals." I didn't add that I wanted George to come over and take a look at things—see what he thought about the visitor. I also wanted to talk to him about a dog. I'd never felt a need to have one around and always thought a dog would be more trouble than help with me often splitting my time between town and country. When I left TJ at the ranch, he lived off the land and did serious mousing in the barn. Besides he frequently absented himself from home several days at a time. I always thought "domesticated' was an oxymoron when describing a cat anyway. A dog, on the other hand, required companionship and regular care.

"Can TJ sleep with me tonight? So I can look after him?"

"As long as he wants to." TJ didn't look like he would raise an objection.

17

Ian

I SAT IN the president's office at the Wainwright Savings Bank, shuffling through a stack of customer notes that were causing me some worry. The notes were unsecured, good as the individual signor's word, which in some cases was not much. The accountant was to meet me here in a half hour. He had spent a week digging through the bank's records and was prepared to render his verdict. I had seen nothing thus far to make me particularly optimistic about the outcome.

It was a lazy Friday afternoon, welcome after a chaotic week. Sunday after church, Mandy and I had enjoyed chicken and gravy and biscuits in the dining room at the Fremont Hotel and afterward had stopped by George Washington's Mount Vernon farm. Mandy stayed at George's to talk with Rosemary while George and I rode over to my place. George had taken a look at TJ who was moving slowly, but didn't seem to mind the attention his injury had brought him. George confirmed that the tabby cat would recover, but was unable to tell whether the blow had been inflicted by man or horse. An examination of the dusty earth behind the corral verified that a human visitor had been the cause of the ruckus at the barn. George had concluded that the party was male and relatively small and had tracked him to the end of the arroyo where a horse had been tethered. We now had a dog at the Lazy Key—a huge gray mongrel that looked like some wolf blood ran in his veins, which might account for the fact that George had named the animal "Wolf." He was an ugly creature, as were most of George's dogs, and he was trained to voice commands, on which George had instructed Mandy, evidently not trusting my memory or my attentiveness to the task.

I had met with the bank's board of directors, and after quickly accomplishing my election as president, explained my concerns about the bank's financial position. I suggested that anyone who was not prepared to weather some tough times should consider resigning. This promptly elicited resignations from the owner of the general store and a livery proprietor, who also served as the town's mayor, neither of whom wanted to risk the public's ire if things went sour. That left Harm Junker, a well-to-do German farmer who was deservedly respected in the farm community and too stubborn to quit anything under pressure, and Amos Thornton, a grizzled grain merchant, who said he was too old to give a damn if trouble came his way. I had correctly anticipated the resignations and immediately elected George Washington and Dr. Theodore Mason, one of the town's two physicians, to fill the slots. Folks seem to love doctors as much as they hate lawyers. Dr. Mason would lend credibility, in addition to his good sense, to the board, and George would bring financial judgment unequalled in Cottonwood County.

Monday would bring Emily Stanton and Casey McGlaun to Borderview. The trial would follow a week or two later. The

Wainwright case was drawing regional attention the likes of which Borderview had never seen.

I continued to review the 'bad note' pile and stopped when I came to one I had not given much thought to before. Isaac Bell. Two thousand dollars. Why in the hell would Ralph loan Ike Bell that kind of money on his signature? There was no way Ike could repay a note that size. As far as I knew he owned nothing but his horse. He lived in a boarding house and the county sheriff's wages were subsistence at best. The note was dated in January six months earlier and payable on demand.

"May I come in, Mr. Locke?" I looked up and saw a cherubic man in a gray wool suit standing in the open doorway, with a bulging briefcase in each hand. I stood and waved him in.

"Be seated, Mr. Tilson. Take off your coat."

Arnold Tilson was a short, bald man closing in on sixty. An accountant who specialized in bank audits, I had used him on several occasions when I needed an independent financial analysis of a banking problem for a client of my former law firm. He worked alone, demanded healthy fees and got them. His voice had an annoying nasal quality, but you got past that quickly when he began to tell the story he had created from his numbers. I considered the man a genius.

Tilson placed his satchels on the floor and removed his coat and put it on the rack in the room's corner. He sat down and methodically began to sort through the papers from one of the bags. I sat back in my own chair and waited patiently, knowing that Tilson preferred to do things in his own way, in his own time.

After some moments, Tilson pushed a sheaf of papers in front of me. "These are the numbers I come up with, Mr. Locke.

Not a very pretty picture. Whether the numbers turn downright ugly depends upon the quality of the bank's assets."

I perused the figures Tilson had entered on the lined paper. The real balance sheet was even worse than the numbers set out in the report. "You're referring to the quality of our notes, I assume."

"Yes. As you can see, the bank has approximately $210,000 in liabilities represented by depositor accounts . . . an impressive amount of deposits, by the way for a community this size, even considering the bank has no competition. On the asset side of the ledger, you have less than $50,000 cash and about $146,000 in borrowers' notes. That gives us a total of some $196,000. Liabilities exceed assets by $14,000 or so . . . if the notes are all good. There is no capital account. It's been sucked dry. The bank's insolvent." He paused and fixed his eyes on mine, blinking like a barn owl. "How good is your note case? I found a goodly number of non-performing loans and way too many unsecured notes, but Mr. Wainwright didn't leave much of an accounting trail. Very few borrower financial statements and little documentation to back up the notes. My past experience tells me, unfortunately, that this is not a hopeful sign. It usually means, Mr. Locke, that much of the paper held by the bank can be relegated to outhouse functions."

I pointed to the stacks of paper on my desk. "A country lawyer knows most of the people in the county. With a few exceptions, I know pretty well who's good for the money and who isn't and who's somewhere in between." I placed my hand on the largest stack. "These are solid loans, not only with assets to back them, but, more importantly, the notes are signed by men who have a high sense of honor. In a few cases, for the protection of the bank and its depositors, we need to request some mortgages to secure the loans, but these are clean. These add up to $112,000 plus. I have another batch here I consider marginal. Mostly small farmers. They're probably okay if it rains in the next week. If it doesn't, I'm afraid half of them go into default. The borrowers are good people, but they're hanging by a thread. We have about $25,000 of these notes." I picked up the remaining stack. "I have $9,000 in notes that can go to the outhouse."

"So," Tilson said, "optimistically, we have a shortfall of about $23,000. I'd add, say, $12,000 of the marginal notes, and you're short $35,000."

"The bad notes and the marginal ones we can charge off to poor judgment or a kind heart, likely some of each."

"Either can be fatal to a banker," Tillson interjected.

I continued. "But according to corporate records the bank has $50,000 in capital stock outstanding. That means that once the bank had at least that much in the capital account even if there weren't any retained profits. Most banks try to build the capital account every year by only paying out a fraction of the profits to shareholders. As near as I can tell, the Wainwright Savings Bank had over $80,000 in the capital account a little more than three years ago. What happened?"

"As you requested, I also audited Mr. Wainwright's personal accounts in the bank. Obviously, I can only ascertain where certain checks were written or when deposits and withdrawals were made, but it isn't all that complicated. Approximately three years ago Mr. Wainwright commenced making large withdrawals from the bank's funds and depositing the money in his personal account. This first wiped out the retained profits, then depleted the equity account and finally wormed its way into the depositors' funds."

"Where was the money going?"

"That wasn't all of it, by the way. He evidently was liquidating personal assets during this time, because there were large deposits from other sources . . . one for some $30,000 a few years back."

I checked my memory for a moment. "Land sale. He sold a section of farmland and another section or more of pasture in Coyote Canyon about that time, all of it in one clean sweep to George Washington. Got clean out of the land business . . . said he was tired of the management headaches."

"Anyway, to answer your question, some of the money is easily tracked. In excess of $75,000 in checks went to one Karl Wainwright during this time. The ledger declared these payments as investments. A relative?"

"Son. Allegedly a real estate investment broker in Kansas City."

Tilson nodded. "Risky business. There were checks to another relative . . . the wife I presume, Celeste Wainwright . . . of something like $20,000. 'Household expenses' these payments were called. A generous household allowance I should say. Fifteen thousand of this was disbursed within the last two months."

"I see." But I didn't.

"Finally, another gentleman enriched himself at Mr. Wainwright's expense: Mr. Isaac Bell, for 'services,' $13,000, more or less. Initially, payments were $250 monthly, but Mr. Bell received $4,000 in April of this year."

"Is that the extent of it?"

"Quite enough I should say, although cash withdrawals from

the personal account amounted to some $10,000 that can't be accounted for."

Gambling, booze, women and Celeste's shopping sprees I surmised, although not necessarily in that order. "How much cash does the bank need, Mr. Tilson?"

Tilson didn't hesitate. "Eighty-four thousand dollars. Fifty thousand dollars to restore the capital stock account. Thirty-four thousand paid into capital to cover the marginal and bad notes. I believe that would restore the soundness of the bank. I wouldn't fear placing my own funds here under those circumstances, provided you had an audit completed annually by an independent accountant and published a summary report of the bank's financial status each year for the benefit of the customers. Only a few banks are starting to do this, but they are finding, I believe, it is in their self-interest to do so. Sophisticated customers, who are, of course, often the largest depositors, are shifting their funds to these banks."

I pondered Tilson's recommendation. I could not dispute it. The bank could cripple along for a while if I could recover enough from Ralph's other assets to infuse cash to cover all of the questionable notes. But what other assets? I was coming face to face with the prospect that Ralph had died a pauper—and that a run on the bank was just a rumor away.

18

Casey

CASEY MCGLAUN OPENED the squeaky door and entered the front room of Ian Locke's law offices. A golden-haired girl was leaning over a typewriter, plunking awkwardly at the keys under the apparent tutelage of a young man. The man turned and straightened upon hearing the door open. His black suit hung on him like rags draped on a scarecrow, Casey thought, but his smooth-cheeked handsomeness was striking, and his dark eyes were limpid pools of gentleness. It was fortunate for the ladies of Borderview this man evidently had no clue he had such charisma and charm. A true innocent.

"Ma'am, can I be of assistance?"

"Yes, I'm Casey McGlaun. I'd like to make an appointment to see Mr. Locke within the next day or so, if possible."

"Miss McGlaun? Yes, of course." The young man stepped toward her. "I'm Will Heasty, Ian's clerk. My pleasure, ma'am. You are something of a celebrity in Cottonwood County."

Casey extended her hand, and Will accepted it clumsily, his face blushing noticeably, but his warm smile extended a genuine welcome. She said, "And this must be Amanda."

The blonde girl, who had been seemingly absorbed with the typewriter, betrayed that she had been more interested in the stranger than she let on, and turned her head toward the visitor. "Folks here call me Mandy. I'm 'Amanda' in Omaha. Should I know you?" Her voice was neutral. The girl was curious, but noncommittal.

"No, but I've heard about you from your father and a mutual friend, Emily Stanton."

Mandy got up from her chair. "You're Mrs. Wainwright's lawyer, aren't you? You're the lady everybody's talking . . . I'm sorry. I guess that's not very polite."

Casey smiled. "That's quite alright, Mandy. I'm not so naïve as to think that a lady lawyer who's defending another lady in a murder case isn't going to be the topic of a few conversations. People have to talk about something, don't they?" Casey deftly shifted the subject. "I see you're becoming a typist."

Mandy shrugged. "Will's teaching me, but I'm not much good yet."

"She's a fast learner," Will interjected. "Two sessions and she's got the keyboard memorized. An unbelievably light touch. She plays piano. I think that has something to do with it."

"I type," Casey said, "but I'm slow as a turtle, and I get very impatient. It's a valuable skill, though, in this age of machines, one that will be a useful tool no matter where life takes you."

"I'd like to be a lawyer," Mandy said. "And a concert violinist or pianist."

"I have a hunch you can be anything you want to be," Casey said.

Locke's office door opened, and Locke stepped out. "Am I missing out on something?"

He saw Casey and she was aware of him appraising her with those smoky, gray eyes. She was slightly annoyed at herself, knowing that she had chosen her favorite cocoa-brown dress in anticipation of a possible meeting with Ian Locke. She did not see the man as a potential romantic interest—she had no time for such distractions—but he was one of the few men who had ever made her feel self-conscious about her attire.

"Hello, Ian," Casey said. "I hope I'm not causing a disruption in your office."

"Casey, this is a surprise."

Locke glided across the room and accepted her proffered hand, holding it a bit longer than necessary, Casey thought. She was uncomfortably aware of his touch, and she shrugged off the feeling.

"I dropped by to make an appointment, Ian. There are a few things I need to discuss with you about my client. Would you have time to see me tomorrow?"

"No. I think not," he said, rubbing his chin thoughtfully.

"Then when?"

Locke responded, "How about now?"

"That would be wonderful. But I don't want to impose."

"No imposition. I've been anxious to talk with you as well . . . about Celeste. Why don't you step into my office?"

"Certainly." Casey turned to Mandy, who had been watching her father and the lady law wrangler with interest. "Mandy, if you don't have other plans, I wonder if you might like to join me for lunch at the Fremont after I meet with your father?"

Mandy looked at her father. "Dad?"

"Sure, Princess. That would be fine. Just remember, afterwards we have to go see Mrs. Beard about piano lessons."

Locke seated Casey next to his desk and then took his own chair. "I understand you've moved in for the duration."

"Yes, I've taken a room at the Fremont. The trial's to commence a week from today. Judge Hutchens will preside. I appreciate you may not be cheering for our success, but I'd welcome anything you can tell me about the judge."

"I'd be glad to help, but first let me say I'm not cheering for anybody when it comes to Celeste's trial. If she's guilty, I hope she's convicted. If she's innocent, I want the jury to acquit. I proceed the same regardless of outcome. Someday, the county judge can decide which will prevails. My immediate concern is to preserve the estate. As to the honorable Conrad Hutchens, I'm glad to share what little I know. I do very little trial work, and, of course, the district court is essentially a trial court. Also, Judge Hutchens serves six counties and doesn't live in Borderview, so we don't see a lot of him."

"I understand he's an older man."

"Mid-sixties. About the age of my father, I guess. Patience is not one of his virtues. His health isn't all that good, and he'll interrupt the trial frequently to make visits to the chamber pot he keeps in the judge's office. I recommend brief opening and closing statements if you want to stay on his good side."

"Brevity is my trademark."

"Unnecessary objections annoy the hell out of him, too. He's kind of a cantankerous old devil, but he has a reputation for fairness. He's known for keeping control of the trial, but he might be a bit obsessed with moving the proceedings along."

"Is he knowledgeable in the law?"

"By reputation, yes. He's not a scholar, and like most lawyers in this part of the country, he clerked his way to the bar examination. He tried a lot of cases in Illinois, and, later, Iowa, before he came to Nebraska right after statehood and latched on to a judgeship. Cyrus Flowers, the county's senior member of the bar, says Hutchens is a lawyer's lawyer. I trust Cy's opinion."

"Your county attorney?"

"First murder case. But he knows his way around the courtroom. He's no man's fool. Very bright. He's never given me cause to doubt his word. Ambitious. Winning this case would give the kind of attention that might get him to the state senate. After that, who knows? Maybe congress. Jess Cooper won't live his life out in Borderview. Too bad. Sooner or later, he'll be corrupted by power."

"Lord Acton."

"Yep. 'Power corrupts. Absolute power corrupts absolutely.' I'm inclined to believe that."

"I won't argue the point. Anyway, I do appreciate your thoughts, Ian."

"There are some other things you should be aware of." Locke told her about the information he had received from Greta Klein, her affair with Ralph and its discovery by Celeste, and the visits by Karl Wainwright and Albert Sweeney to the Wainwright mansion. "I've shared this with the county attorney. I haven't learned any of this information as the result of confidential communications, and I'm obligated, as an officer of the court, to disclose."

Casey's expression was intense. "Some of this comes as a surprise. Not all. I'm grateful for your candor. I don't like being blindsided."

"One other thing. I may be able to tell you more before trial, but for the moment, I can't give you any facts to backup what I say. Just keep your eye on Sheriff Bell. He's deeply entangled with the Wainwright family. I don't know the extent of his involvement yet, but he's a piece of the puzzle."

"I'll remember that. And now I'd better take my leave. I have a young lady waiting to join me for lunch."

Locke arose to see Casey to the door. "I'm curious. You just met Mandy. I find it interesting you invited her to lunch. Any particular reason?"

Casey bristled and whirled to face him. "Do I need a reason?"

Locke raised his hands in mock surrender. "Now I know why curiosity killed a cat. Irish temper. No, you don't need a reason. Peace offering. Emily's coming out to my ranch for the day Saturday. I asked her if she thought you might be persuaded to accompany her. She said you might if I asked nicely. I'm asking nicely."

Casey met his gaze evenly and saw the twinkle in his eyes. Her annoyance melted. "Okay . . . if I can take the time away from the case."

19

Casey

CASEY AND MANDY sat at a small table in the Fremont Hotel's dining room, as the waiter served each a large plate of roast beef and boiled potatoes smothered with rich gravy. "I'll bring your apple pie later, ladies. Let me know if you need anything else in the meantime."

Casey was delighted to note that Mandy shared her healthy appetite. Friends sometimes teased her about her eating capacity, and, while she took it good naturedly, she was occasionally self-conscious about the portions she consumed. Gratefully, she never gained a pound and was unencumbered by the confining corsets most of her contemporaries endured.

Mandy seemed remarkably at ease with this comparative stranger, Casey observed, her poise far greater than her own at eleven years. Of course, she had no doubt dined in many far more elegant places in the society she traveled with in the big city. Casey chided herself for her abrupt reaction to Ian's query when she was departing his office. She supposed it was because her motives were not entirely noble. She had invited Mandy to lunch, not only because she seemed like such an interesting girl, but also for the reason she sensed a loneliness—no, it was more a fragile vulnerability—hidden beneath the polished veneer of her self-assurance and seeming placidity. She had impulsively decided this girl might need a friend, but she also had to admit Mandy had piqued her curiosity. It seemed the Lockes had a way of doing that.

"Are you enjoying your stay here, Mandy?" The first clumsy effort to ignite a conversation.

Mandy looked up. Such incredible blue eyes. Not her father's color, but the look was there, like she saw things others did not. Mandy studied Casey for some moments, evidently sizing up her luncheon companion, deciding how much of herself she should expose to this stranger. "I like it here," she said. "More than I ever dreamed. I gave Dad a terrible time about coming to Borderview . . . but that was mostly because I wasn't given a choice. I always wanted to see where he lived. Don't tell him, though." She grinned conspiratorially.

"Do you spend a lot of time in his office?"

Mandy precisely and properly sliced her beef, took a bite, chewed and swallowed before she spoke. "Not a lot. I ride into town with Dad two days a week. I run errands. Do filing. And then, Will's teaching me to type. I'll be taking piano lessons, too, on the days I'm in town. Most other days I'm at my friend Rosemary's. I stay there overnight if Dad has to be in town to work. Weekends we're both usually home. George . . . he's Dad's best friend . . . says Dad wasn't at the ranch much before I came to visit."

"You said you'd like to be a concert pianist. Have you played for a long time?"

"I can't remember when I didn't. I play violin, too. I give

Mother credit for my musical interests. She started me on lessons when I was very small, and it came pretty easy to me, I guess. But if you want to be good at it, there's nothing easy about that. It's practice, practice, practice. Sometimes at home I play for hours . . . Mozart, Chopin, Schubert . . . and I'm in a world of my own where there's no pain and everybody's happy. About being a concert pianist or violinist though—"

"Yes?"

"I fibbed. That's what Mother wants . . . if I can't find a rich husband. I really want to be a lawyer. It's in the Locke blood, you know. The Lockes can't help it. Dad says it's like a disease. I think I caught it at Dad's office. Don't tell him, though. I don't think he wants that for me. He'll need time to get used to the idea."

Casey laughed. "It's not a terrible thing. I can't imagine not being a lawyer. There's a challenge waiting every waking moment. I get to surround myself with books. And nothing compares to the excitement of the courtroom. I think you'd be a great lawyer. But don't tell your father I said so."

"Dad likes you."

Casey was taken aback. "Well, I hope so. I haven't known him long, but I'd hate to think he dislikes me."

"That's not what I mean. He . . . he's fascinated by you. I saw the way he looked at you this morning. I've never seen him look at anybody else like that. Actually, it seemed kind of rude to me, but he didn't mean it that way."

Casey changed the subject. "Your father's invited me to spend the day at your ranch Saturday. Emily Stanton and I will rent a buggy at the livery and ride out together."

"That's wonderful. Dad and I are going to demonstrate our culinary skills. We're going to make everything in Dutch ovens . . . beef stew, cobbler."

"I can hardly wait."

"Do you ride horses?"

"I was born on a horse. My father was a cavalry sergeant. He had me riding before I was walking."

"Maybe we could go riding Saturday."

"That's the best idea I've heard for a long time."

Mandy wrinkled her brow thoughtfully. "There's a problem, though."

"What's that?"

"We only have two saddle horses . . . my mare, Dancer, and old Hemlock."

"Can't I ride Hemlock?"

"You'd have to ask Dad. He won't let me ride him, because he's too mean and contrary."

"I'll deal with Hemlock . . . and your father."

20

Ian

WE DID NOT have a directors' room or conference table at the Wainwright Savings Bank, so the grim-faced men who ostensibly governed the bank and more or less controlled its destiny had to meet in the cramped space of the less than grandiose president's office. Whatever extravagances Ralph might have engaged in, he had not showered them upon the bank facilities. Perhaps, he thought, trappings of prosperity would have been resented by the customers.

I waited silently while the four directors shuffled through Tilson's financial reports. A few of the men might not fully understand, but they would grasp the stark realities of the bottom line. The Wainwright Savings Bank was teetering on the edge of an abyss that would financially destroy half of Cottonwood County's residents if it tipped the wrong way.

"Shit," mumbled Amos Thornton, "how in the hell did this happen? I didn't see anything like this coming. Ralph always said this place was going like a dancing devil. Said he was piling up money like corn after a banner harvest. 'Course we never asked no questions. Directors' checks kept getting bigger and figured that was a sure sign the bank was doing real good."

I didn't tell the old man that the hefty directors' fees were subtle bribes to assure the directors asked no questions. The men had the best of intentions; they were just naïve. I had no reservations about the honesty of any of the directors, even those who resigned.

Thornton was a small, toothpick of a man in his seventies with crisscrosses of wrinkles etched deeply in his face. He was a tough old bird and I knew he had stayed on because it wasn't in him to run from a fight. He shook his head. "Can't let the bank go down."

"Ja," said Harm Junker, a husky farmer with a wind-burnt face. "It would not be my end, but my brothers and many of mein neighbors would not be able to stand up to this. What must we do?" Junker's pale, blue eyes fixed on me. "Tell us about this trouble, Ian, in a way we can understand."

I looked at George, whose stone face betrayed nothing, and then at Dr. Mason, a trim man with snow-white hair and moustache who was a few years shy of his fiftieth birthday. Mason nodded thoughtfully. "Spread the cards on the table, Ian."

I briefly summarized Arnold Tilson's financial reports and my evaluation of the bank's note inventory. "The bottom line, gentlemen, is that the bank needs about $84,000 if we're going to do more than just staunch the bleeding."

A heavy silence settled on the room. Finally, Thornton spoke. "So Ralph sold his last saddle. Can't the bank get some of the money back from his estate?

I replied, "I'm special administrator for Ralph's estate, which makes me responsible for collecting all of his assets and paying his bills until a will's probated and an executor takes over. The problem I have here is that Ralph owned one hundred per cent of the bank's stock, so the only shareholder he would be liable to would be himself. Since the bank was incorporated, individual shareholders are not ordinarily liable for a bank's debt. Arguably, Ralph improperly managed the depositors' funds, but this would likely require lawsuits against the estate by individual depositors to recover any shortfalls . . . that's after the bank's already gone under. That also assumes there are funds to recover from the estate."

"You telling us Ralph had empty pockets?" Thornton asked.

"That's a distinct possibility. It seems probable, in any event, the estate wouldn't come close to covering any shortage."

"Who all is aware of this?" asked Dr. Mason.

"As near as I know, just the men in this room. But I'll have to file an inventory with the court soon, and then it will be a public record."

"And an hour later, there will be a run on the bank," Mason said softly.

Junker shook his head in disbelief. For a man who had scrimped and worked his way to financial success, he likely could not comprehend the idea that a man would play as loose with his money as Ralph had. He said, "Well, Ian, what do you want us to do?"

I looked around the room, trying to read the somber faces of the board members. George's face was impassive, revealing nothing. The others could not hide their worry and bewilderment. "One option is to close the bank immediately . . . before a run. If the bank's going to fail, it would be fairest to all the customers if we just locked up. This way, nobody would have an advantage over anybody else. We'd pro-rate the cash among the depositors and hope to collect on some of the notes and throw that into the pot eventually . . . but there would be no more bank."

Mason said, "You seem to be implying there's another option."

"There is. Put together some investors to buy the bank stock from the estate. I'd have to get court approval, but I'd propose to sell Ralph's 50,000 shares to the investors for a dollar a share, with an agreement they would pay the $50,000 into the bank to restore the equity account and another $35,000 to the surplus account to cover any bad notes . . . and they'd have to agree to release the estate from further liability. This would save the bank and clean up a nasty problem for the estate."

Thornton twisted his face and focused his eyes on rolling a cigarette. "Why would any damn fool want to buy in to this game?"

"Profit."

"Profit? You're telling us the goddamn bank's near busted, and there's still money to be made here?"

"Absolutely. It's fairly simple actually. Ralph was pulling out $25,000 a year in salary and profits besides raiding the capital accounts. That's one hell of a lot of money. If investors put $84,000 into the stock and surplus account, most of it's not seriously at risk. Some of the surplus is going to slip away on bad notes, maybe a bunch if it doesn't rain. That's where the risk is. But the new shareholders and directors can hire a good man to run the bank . . . be the president . . . for $10,000. That leaves the other $15,000 for dividends or increased surplus for expansion. This assumes the bank doesn't grow. With the right kind of management, I think this bank could double or triple in size.

Tilson had some excellent ideas that would encourage large depositors. A lot of the money around here goes out of county. How many of you have all of your funds in Wainwright Savings Bank?"

There was no response. I continued. "This county has some wealthy men who don't drop a dime here. The bank needs to be able to assure those folks their money's safe and somebody needs to ask for their deposits. Ralph never made any effort to round up business."

Dr. Mason folded his arms and leaned back in his chair. "Ian, it sounds to me like you've been giving this a lot of thought. Your enthusiasm doesn't seem to be with the closing option."

"I won't deny it. I don't want to see the bank fail. I don't want to be a part of that. But if the investors can't make a profit, the bank will go under sooner or later anyway. Some dimwitted folks cuss profit, but I've never seen anybody stay in business and provide jobs or merchandise or services without profits. I wouldn't want my funds in a bank that lost money."

Mason said, "I'm not a wealthy man, but I could raise enough to put up ten percent . . . $8,500."

Junker nodded. "I could do that, but I would risk no more."

"Count me in for $8,500," said Thornton.

I still owed on the ranch mortgage, but I could borrow more on the place. Also, it occurred to me Cam might find the proposition interesting. Anyway, I had brought up the idea. Time to put my money with my mouth. "I'd go for ten percent, but I might need to let my brother, Cam, in on my share. Also, I'd have to ask the court to approve my participation, because I have a potential conflict of interest with my responsibility to the estate."

All eyes turned to George Washington, who had yet to offer

a single word. "I'll take the rest of it," he said, "with one condition."

"What's the condition?" I asked.

"That you will serve as president of the bank for at least one year."

I was taken aback. George's condition had not been a part of my calculations.

"I don't know if I can do that. I'm not sure I can just abandon my law practice."

I turned to the other board members. "What do the rest of you think about my running the bank?"

Dr. Mason said, "Ian, it doesn't really matter. As I understand it, each share has one vote. George will have sixty percent of the votes. He's going to have the say-so about how the bank is run. But for what it's worth, I think it's an excellent idea."

"Ja," said Junker.

"Yep," said Thornton.

21

Ian

I SEARCHED THE horizon for some sign of Mandy and Casey. Over my protests, Casey had insisted upon saddling Hemlock and joining Mandy for a ride to the Little Blue River some three miles east of the Lazy Key. Somewhat to my annoyance, Hemlock had been docile as a child's pony under Casey's tutelage and given total lie to his reputation as a tyrant. I was beginning to take the gelding's contrary behavior personally.

Mandy and Casey had galloped out of the ranch yard faster than good sense dictated, and this had been cause for some apprehension on my part. Casey had shown a daring, wild side since her arrival with Emily in the rented buggy. She had presented herself ready for a day outdoors, attired in a yellow cotton shirt and blue dungarees, boys' garments she had purchased at Carpenter's Dry Goods Emporium. Her well-worn boots had evidently traveled with her from a past that did not involve the courtroom. All in all, I had to admit she was every bit as striking, if not more so, in her outdoor garb, as in the quality, tailored gowns and dresses she usually wore. Her feminine curves stretched the boys' garments a bit, and lecher that I am, I duly noted the press of small, firm, and apparently unencumbered, breasts against the soft fabric of her shirt.

The farmstead had come alive at Casey's appearance. Mandy had rushed out to greet the visitors, Wolf warmed to Casey instantly, and even TJ plumped into her lap as soon as she took a seat on the porch step. After watering and graining the buggy horse, I returned to my domestic tasks, laying logs in the outdoor fire pit to prepare a bed of coals for the Dutch ovens—too damned hot to cook indoors. Emily had found a spot in the shade of a nearby oak with Whitman's *Leaves of Grass* for companionship, while Mandy introduced Casey to the horses and critters. The camaraderie between the two appeared genuine, and that somehow pleased me. Their interaction was relaxed and natural, and from a distance they looked like two girls engaged in animated conversation, although in this instance the true girl was an inch or two taller than the woman.

I pulled out my pocket watch and observed that the riders had been out nearly two hours. I had told them the chuck wagon opened at one o'clock, which was a half hour away. I hoped Casey's reversion to childhood did not include obliviousness to time. The clock and I are rarely parted, and I am inclined to be unforgiving about unexcused tardiness. I checked the stew simmering in the oven, shards of beef, large chunks of potatoes, a healthy contribution of green beans and carrots, and a smaller contingent of diced tomatoes and peppers. I had raspberry cobbler baking in one of the ovens and had another ready to receive biscuits as soon all of the guests returned.

"Smells scrumptious."

I started at the sound of Emily's voice, so absorbed had I been in my cooking chores. I got up from my knees and gave her a hug. "Yes, if the taste rises up to the aroma, we'll eat quite well today, if I may say so myself."

"I wasn't aware you had such culinary talents."

I smiled. "Culinary. Mandy's favorite new word. Yes, I've had to hone my cooking skills since Mandy came here. She's getting quite handy in the kitchen herself."

"She seems happy."

"Most of the time. But sometimes she descends into dark moods and long periods of silence. As if she's been overwhelmed by a deep sadness."

"It could just be she's growing up. At a certain age girls become prone to moodiness . . . or she could just be her father's child." She nudged me gently in the ribs.

"It's more than that," I insisted.

"Be patient. She seems quite smitten by Casey. I think that's a good thing."

"I hope so. Casey's something of an enigma to me."

"Interesting."

"What do you mean?"

"On our way out, Casey said the same thing about you. Exact same words."

"Is that so?"

"Yes, that's so. I highly recommend you both quit trying to appraise each other like a couple of law wranglers readying to do battle in the courtroom. Forget you're lawyers. I told her the same thing."

I pulled out my watch again. "It's fifteen minutes till one. I hope they haven't run into trouble."

"What kind of trouble could they possibly encounter? You worry too much, Ian."

I had not told Emily about the recent visitor. There seemed no point. But I had been keeping a close eye on Mandy's whereabouts, and I did worry when she was out of sight for long.

"Besides," Emily said, "Mandy couldn't be under better care. Casey McGlaun can take care of both of them quite handily. She was raised in west Texas before civilization even came close. She lived with the Comanche for nearly two years, you know."

Emily's remark got my attention. "I didn't know."

"She was a captive. She and her mother were traveling in a small wagon train without military escort on their way to Fort Bliss to join her father when they were attacked by a Comanche war party. Casey was the only survivor. She was twelve at the time, and the Comanche occasionally took white children and raised them as their own. Quanah Parker, the chief of this particular band, himself was the son of a white woman who had been taken captive. Anyway, one of the braves was especially taken with her red hair, according to Casey, and he claimed her for himself. She lived with his family until she was nearly fourteen." She hesitated. "I don't know if I should be saying this. Casey doesn't talk about her experience much, but she doesn't treat it as a deep, dark secret, either. The past is relevant to Casey only for its lessons, I'd guess."

I left it to Emily to decide whether to continue.

"Shortly before her fourteenth birthday, the brave who had saved her took her as his third wife. During the third week of their marriage, Casey made herself a widow when she cut the brave's throat while he slept and then she escaped into the night."

"Jesus."

"A day later she stumbled upon a cavalry patrol and was

eventually reunited with her father at Fort Bliss. She lived on post there for three years until her father was transferred to Fort Sill in Oklahoma Territory. He died there a year or so later, and Casey moved on to Colorado. Believe me, her life story would make quite a book. But so would yours."

"I suspect there's a book in each person's life . . . even yours, Emily Stanton."

Emily pointed to the knoll some one hundred yards distant that sloped toward the ranch yard. "You can put on your biscuits, Ian, the wayward riders are returning . . . right on schedule, I should say."

We had dinner at a table I set up on the veranda, and healthy appetites cleaned up most of the contents of the Dutch ovens. My guests seemed to genuinely appreciate the simple fare, and I accepted compliments graciously, and with some pride, I should add. Everybody pitched in with the cleanup, and I savored the good-natured banter that made the chore so pleasant. Solitude was most of my incentive for living on the ranch, but I did not mind the female companionship a bit. A man could get accustomed to it.

We lazed on the porch and chatted for a while after the dishes were put away. Then Emily suggested she and Mandy play dominoes while Casey and I take a walk. "Show Casey the weeping springs," Emily said.

Casey and I looked at each other. Casey rolled her eyes and I shrugged and lifted myself from the comfortable rocker. "If Casey's not too tired."

Rising quickly to the challenge, Casey said, "I need to stretch my legs after a morning in the saddle."

We strolled leisurely away from the ranch house and made

our way into the arroyo behind the barn, following the cow trail there toward the far southwest corner of the pasture. "You had a good ride this morning?" I asked, trying to make conversation.

"Perfect. I hadn't ridden since spring, and I loved it. Hemlock's a magnificent animal. Wherever did you find him?"

"My brother, Cam, gave him to me. Cam raises Appaloosas. Frankly, Hemlock and I don't get along so well, and I was never sure that Cam didn't just shuck one of his troublemakers off on me. You seemed to have him charmed, though."

"I've always been able to handle most horses . . . and then I spent some time with the Comanche. Did Emily mention that?"

"She did, in passing."

"They're the greatest horsemen who ever lived, and the horses were the best of my experience there."

"It must have been terrifying."

"At first. But I decided I wanted to live, so I adapted and learned their ways, their language. When I quit trying to run away and stopped crying every time someone came near, they began to treat me as one of their own. I never gave up the idea of escaping, but I also made up my mind to be happy if I ended up living out my life there. I came to love many of the people, and I still wonder what has become of some of them. I know Quanah lives near Fort Sill with his seven or eight wives and is said to be taking up the white man's ways. He is a charismatic leader, and he will survive. I might have stayed for many years if the brave who had taken me as a wife had not beaten me to within an inch of my life. I chose not to give him a second opportunity."

"You were very brave, I'd say."

"I did what I had to do."

"I understand that."

"Yes, you were in the war. I suppose you do. I think living with the Comanche would be greatly preferable to Gettysburg."

I changed the subject. "Did you and Mandy get as far as the Little Blue?"

"Oh yes. It's a lovely river. I see the source of its name. The water runs so clear over the sandy riverbed it looks like a huge blue ribbon. While we were there, something happened I thought I should mention."

"What's that?"

"While we rode along the river bank, I had a feeling we were being watched. I can't explain it. The hair just bristled on the back of my neck. I didn't say anything to Mandy but gradually let her get out ahead of me some distance. Then I dismounted and watched and waited. In a few minutes I heard movement in the woods and drew my pistol. He must have thought I had spotted him, because whoever it was took off like a fresh branded calf. I would have gone after him, but I didn't want to leave Mandy alone . . . especially if things didn't go my way."

"You had a gun?"

"Smith & Wesson Russian model, six inch barrel. It's very accurate, not terribly heavy. I carry it in my possible sack or hand bag. Why would someone be following us?"

"I honestly don't know." I told her about the prowler at the ranch. "Can you describe the man?"

"Not close enough to get a good look. Smaller than average. Wide brimmed hat. Green shirt and gray trousers. Dressed a bit nicely for a stroll in the countryside. Ian, if he is the same man that was at your place last week, he wasn't following me."

"I know."

As the arroyo faded into the flatter grasslands, we came to a translucent stream that tumbled over the sandstone sluice it had carved in a twisted path through the once lush meadows of my pasture. A few cows with calves at side were drinking at the stream and looked at us curiously.

"Herefords," Casey remarked. "They're taking over cow country, aren't they?"

"Yes. But if it doesn't rain soon, I'll have to cull the herd mercilessly." I gestured toward the dry, brown carpet that lined the stream. "They've about grubbed the grass to its roots."

"At least you've got water."

"Yes, that's why I bought this place. Water. The windmill near the house pumps from a well that's never been close to dry. And this stream is spring fed from a source on my land. This way." I motioned her to head upstream.

In a matter of minutes our trek turned up a steep slope, at the top of which was an enormous outcropping of sandstone, the most prominent of which was shaped like a giant mushroom. A scattering of oak and cottonwood furnished an oasis of shade for the area. As we reached the outcropping, the stream dead-ended into a wide clear pool, at the far end of which was a sandstone wall. Water trickled from the porous rock as though passing through a sieve, but most prominent on the wall were two parallel holes some three feet apart from which slowly poured rivulets of spring water.

I said, "Some folks say those two holes in the rock look like big eyes if you use imagination . . . thus, 'Weeping Springs.' The sandstone formation above is known hereabouts as 'Mushroom Rock.'"

Casey seemed mesmerized by the scene, as her eyes took in what I sometimes called my little Garden of Eden. "I've never seen a place more breathtaking," she said. "Even in this drought, it perseveres."

"Take off your boots and cool your feet. Take a drink from one of the eyes. There's no colder, sweeter water on this earth."

We slipped off our boots, rolled up our pant legs and waded into the pool, which was no more than two feet at the deepest. We drank lustily from nature's fountains, soaked our feet for a spell and then rested in the shade with backs propped against tree trunks. We talked for several hours, even the old clockmeister losing track of the time. There was something about this place and this time that opened us both up. First, there were the little, insignificant disclosures as we tiptoed our ways up the fragile stairway that leads to trust, but by the end of our time there I had revealed parts of myself I had never displayed to another person, not even Emily or Cam. I do not think I flatter myself when I say Casey must have done the same. I warned myself that I was on treacherous footing here and that Casey would be returning to another life when Celeste's trial was over. Still, when finally and reluctantly we picked ourselves up and headed back to the house, I admitted to myself that I was incapable of shrugging off my fascination with this woman.

22

Casey

CASEY MCGLAUN WAITED in the makeshift courtroom that doubled as a town hall. The room was a large, hollow shell in final stages of construction, and the scent of fresh-sawn lumber wafted in the air. Seating for spectators consisted of temporary benches constructed of cedar planks and limestone blocks. Tables and chairs for judge and counsel had been moved from the county courtroom across the street, and jury chairs had been commandeered from other county offices. Because of the notoriety of the trial, District Judge Conrad Hutchens had pressed the hall into service to accommodate the rafts of newspaper reporters and onlookers expected to pack the room. Ordinarily, pending construction of a courthouse on the town square, district court matters were taken up in the county courtroom, which could not hold a jury much less the hordes of spectators who had already begun to file into the austere room.

The meat of the trial commenced today, and Casey had chosen a gray, high-necked dress, no less conservative than the black one she had worn yesterday for jury selection and opening statements. She dared not risk offending any of the upright males on the jury, some of whom might be wary of a female advocate in any case. Celeste had rebelled at Casey's instructions to dress similarly, but in a test of wills, Casey had gone to the Wainwright mansion and personally selected Celeste's garments and had bluntly informed Celeste she had no choice, since her lawyer was her only link to the wardrobe. Casey had no intention of letting her client steer the case.

The *voir dire* had gone well enough, and examination of the all-male jury pool had identified the worst prospects from Casey's perspective, and she had whittled them from the jury, first by motions for cause—such as friendship with a witness or other reasons for possible bias—and then via her six peremptory challenges. The latter allowed her to strike potential jurors she decided by logic or instinct were, from her client's standpoint, best removed. Jury selection could be tedious, but Casey was satisfied with the work that had pared the prospects to twelve tried and true. She was particularly pleased to have targeted two jurors to whom her message would be directed. One was a smooth-cheeked schoolmarm, obviously sincere and bright, eager to do his duty. The other was a burley blacksmith, who had seemed fair-minded during *voir dire* and unsusceptible to intimidation. She saw each man as a different kind of leader whose influence could sway others, or who, if persuaded of the rightness of his view, would hold out and deny the required unanimous verdict to convict, plummeting the case into mistrial.

Each lawyer had made opening statements following jury selection, and Casey was reasonably comfortable with her own ten minutes of remarks, which, if nothing else, had elicited a collective sigh of relief from judge and jury after Jess Cooper's one hour opening. Today the prosecutor would begin to lay his evidence before the jury, and Casey felt butterflies in her stomach as trial approached. She had the experience now to know, however, this was a good sign, that her nervousness only meant she was ready for the race.

Jess Cooper entered the building and took his place at the opposing counsel table. He nodded pleasantly, and Casey returned the greeting. Momentarily, the sheriff escorted Celeste Wainwright to her chair next to Casey's. The woman was incapable of looking anything but regal, Casey thought.

"Good morning, Celeste," Casey said. "Did you rest well last night?'

"Of course. You said I should put this in your hands. I have taken your words to heart." A tad bit of sarcasm, perhaps?

A rotund court reporter with pens, ink and a stack of paper took a chair at the left far end of the judge's table, which had been placed on a wooden platform to give the jurist some semblance of an elevated bench. Abruptly, the bailiff announced, "All rise."

The room's occupants arose as one, and District Judge Conrad Hutchens limped through the back door of the building and made his way to the judge's table. A pale man, whose black robe could not hide a rail-thin body, the judge appeared frail and sickly. But his voice was strong, and, with his command of the courtroom and eminent fairness, he had already earned Casey's respect.

The judge set his reading glasses on the table and looked sternly at the lawyers. "Are you ready to proceed, counsel?"

Both replied, "Yes, your Honor."

"Then, Mr. Cooper, the prosecution may commence its case."

"Very well, your Honor. The prosecution calls Sheriff Isaac

Bell."

Ike Bell swaggered to the judge's table and was sworn by Judge Hutchens before he took a straight-back chair in front of the court reporter. The county attorney stood and rattled off a series of mundane questions to establish the sheriff's professional qualifications, and Bell responded quickly and confidently. That accomplished, Cooper commenced his examination.

"Sheriff Bell, were you acquainted with Ralph Wainwright?"

"Yes, sir. Knowed him since statehood."

"And when did you last see Mr. Wainwright?"

"Dead or alive?"

"Deceased."

"Well, I seen him in Tillie Crump's pigpen this past June."

Cooper sighed. "Would that have been June 8, 1884 to be more precise?"

Cooper glanced at Casey, anticipating an objection. He was blatantly leading the witness, but it was pointless to object, Casey thought. The answers were irrelevant to guilt or innocence, and it would serve only to annoy the judge and the jury to interrupt with repeated objections. Save them for when it counted.

The sheriff responded. "Yes sir, June 8. That was the date."

"Can you tell the jury in your own words how you came to be there and what you found?"

"Well, I come to be there because Ian Locke rides up to my place that afternoon and says him and Tillie found Ralph's body in the pigpen. I rounded up my deputy, little Jimmy Hawkins, and Cash Berry, the undertaker, and headed out to Tillie's like a Kansas tornado. Hell, you come along later. You know we was there."

"And what did you find at Tillie Crump's?"

"We found Ralph's head, one foot, an arm and other sundry parts?"

"You found the dead body of Ralph Wainwright?"

"Never saw a live head by itself. As to a body, there wasn't much, but I can swear that Ralph had cashed in his chips."

A tittering arose from the spectators, and the reporters began writing feverishly. The sheriff promised to add a bit of color to this trial. The judge tapped his gavel a few times on the table and quieted the crowd with a glare.

Cooper continued. "Sheriff, did you observe anything about Mr. Wainwright's remains that caused you to suspect foul play?"

The sheriff was obviously relishing his moment in the public eye and was playing to the audience now. "Well, a man don't just jump in a pigpen and offer himself up for supper."

The spectators laughed loudly, and the judge hammered his gavel repeatedly on the table. First, the judge admonished Ike Bell. "Sheriff, this is a most serious matter. You are in this courtroom as an officer of the law, and I expect your responses to be made with appropriate dignity. You are the county sheriff, not the county clown."

The sheriff's face reddened, and the judge faced the spectators. "There will be no more outbursts. Next time, I clear the courtroom. Continue, Mr. Cooper."

Casey did not envy the county attorney. A witness out of control was a living nightmare. Either Cooper had not coached his witness or the witness was impervious to coaching, likely the latter.

The county attorney rephrased his earlier question. "Sheriff Bell, was there anything specific about the condition of Mr. Wainwright's remains to cause you to conclude he was murdered?"

"Yes, sir. There was a bullet hole in his skull."

Casey arose from her chair. "Objection, your Honor. The prosecution has offered no evidence to show the witness's competency to testify on this issue or the basis for him to draw such a conclusion."

The judge removed his eyeglasses and rubbed his eyes thoughtfully. "Sustained," he said. "The jury will disregard the witness's answer."

Cooper tried again. "Sheriff, in your experience as a lawman, have you had occasion to observe a number of bullet wounds?"

"Yes sir."

"And can you describe the condition of Mr. Wainwright's skull that persuaded you he had been struck with a bullet?"

"Well, I don't know what else would have made a hole like that."

Cooper flinched, waiting for Casey's objection. She decided she would rather demolish the testimony than exclude it, especially since she doubted the jury's collective ability to truly disregard anything said in the courtroom. She considered objections more a tool to keep opposing counsel honest than anything else.

Cooper directed another question to his witness. "Was there anything about the hole in the skull that, based upon your experience, would convince you that this was a bullet hole?"

"The size. It was a little hole. Nothing else could make a hole like that."

The county attorney moved on with his examination, squeezing a clumsy narrative from the sheriff supervising the removal of the remains from the Crump farm to Cash Berry's funeral parlor. Casey allowed Cooper to lead the sheriff through the story without objection, but her vigilance intensified when the prosecutor's questions took a sudden turn in another direction.

"Sheriff," Cooper said, "I want to ask you about something that happened subsequent to the discovery of Mr. Wainwright's body. Is it true that someone approached you with information about the circumstances of Mr. Wainwright's death?"

"Yes, sir. His son. Mr. Karl Wainwright."

"And what did he tell you about those circumstances?"

That son of a bitch. "Objection, your Honor. That question calls for blatant hearsay. It relies totally upon the statements of another party, not upon anything within the personal knowledge of this witness. The sheriff cannot testify about anything told to him by another party, who as a matter of fact is on the prosecution's witness list."

"Sustained," said the judge. "This line of questioning is improper Mr. Cooper."

Cooper shrugged innocently and sat down. "The state has no further questions of this witness."

The judge said. "Before cross, Miss McGlaun, I'm going to call a ten minute recess. The witness may step down if he wishes."

During the recess, Casey reviewed her notes, however, she fumed silently at Cooper's attempt to get the hearsay testimony past her. How stupid did he think she was? She was more insulted than anything else. She supposed he was testing her, and maybe that was fair enough, but she had an aversion to approaching law as a game. She took a deep breath and let her temper cool. Anger in the courtroom could blind a trial lawyer at a critical moment. She looked up from her notes for a moment, just long enough to see Ian Locke slip into the room and claim an abandoned chair at the back of the room.

"You like him, don't you?"

Casey turned to Celeste, who had evidently been watching her. "Ian Locke? I find him an interesting man. He has an enviable reputation as a lawyer in this community." She wasn't interested in sharing any thoughts about Ian with a woman who had, during an interview at the jail, flaunted the fact she was his former lover.

"I would have married him if he'd asked me," Celeste said almost wistfully. "He was mine for a time, but he didn't love me, not in the marrying way."

Casey did not comment and returned to her notes. In a few moments, Judge Hutchens took his seat and a more subdued Sheriff Bell made his way to the witness chair.

The judge declared the court reconvened and nodded at Casey. "You may proceed with cross, counselor."

Casey stood and moved deliberately around the table to approach the witness, who, unable to meet her penetrating gaze, cast his eyes downward. "Sheriff Bell," she said, "you testified that when you were at the Crump farm you observed a bullet wound in the skull of the deceased, is that correct?"

"Yes, ma'am."

"And in reference to this hole—" Casey walked to her table, picked up a sheet of parchment and appeared to be studying it thoughtfully, as she turned back to Bell. "You stated you didn't know what else would have made a hole like that. Am I quoting you accurately?"

The sheriff shrugged nervously. "I suppose so, more or less."

"More or less?"

"I said what you said I said," Bell growled testily.

"Just how would you describe this wound in the deceased's head? I don't recall that you ever answered this question when Mr. Cooper posed it, other than to say it was a 'little' hole."

"It was a little hole, like I said."

"A little hole." Casey's brow furrowed as if trying to understand. "How little? The size of a penny?"

"Bigger than that."

"The size of a silver dollar?"

"Some bigger."

Casey made a circle with her thumbs and forefingers and raised her hands in the direction of the jury. "This big, Sheriff?"

"Almost, I guess."

Casey whirled back to the witness. "My word, Sheriff are you suggesting someone shot Mr. Wainwright with a cannon?"

Bell flushed with anger. "No, of course not."

"A buffalo gun?"

"No."

"What kind of a weapon would make a hole that size?"

"I can't say."

"You can't say? But I believe it has been implied that you have some expertise in such matters."

"I've been a lawman a good many years."

"Yes, I recall you testified to that. How many murders have you investigated in the eight years you have served as sheriff of this county?"

"Uh, I'm not exactly sure."

"Would it be fair to say, Sheriff, that there has been only one murder in this county during your tenure?"

"My what?"

"Your years of service."

"I guess maybe there ain't been more than one. I run a law-abiding county here. We've had two folks do themselves in though."

"Was not one of those suicides by hanging?"

"Well, yeah, but the other shot hisself."

"With what?"

"Swallowed a shotgun."

"And the single murder case. Was that crime solved?"

"Uh . . . no."

Casey was silent for a moment, allowing time for the jury to sort out the sheriff's testimony. She returned to her table on the pretense of reviewing her notes again. When she turned back to Bell, she observed that he was looking haggard and solemn, ready to call it a day.

"Sheriff, I have just a few more questions. If I were to ask you to characterize this so-called bullet hole as round or ragged, what would be your reply?"

"Ragged, I suppose. Things was pretty tore up."

"Reconsidering your previous testimony, could you concede just the slightest possibility that something other than a bullet could have caused this damage . . . a sharp instrument, even a hammer, perhaps?"

"Well, maybe possible, but not likely."

Casey returned to her seat. "No further questions, your Honor."

23

Ian

"WHICH WAY DO you think the wind's blowing?" Will Heasty asked, referring to the progress of the Wainwright trial.

We were seated in my office weighing some of the events that were forcing us to decisions that neither of us had expected to face prior to the anticipated verdict in Celeste's trial. I had just returned from observing a few hours of the first full day of the trial. The judge had declared a recess for lunch and I had grabbed a sandwich at Reuben's before returning to the office to meet with Will.

"Can't tell at this point," I said. "Casey made chopped beef out of Ike's testimony. She's damned good . . . smooth as silk. She never asks a question she doesn't pretty much know the answer to. She's not going to choke on any of her own words. Jess is a good enough lawyer, but he sure as hell better have some solid facts on his side."

"What's happening this afternoon?"

"Jess is calling Cash Berry and Doc Hesterman, I guess. Still trying to establish cause of death. I can't imagine Cash would add much that couldn't be pretty well shredded by the defense.

Doc might do the prosecution some good, but I have a hunch Casey's physician out of Omaha gave her reason to believe cause can't be proved. And he's always in the background as an expert for the defense. If there's a credible eyewitness, it seems to me that most of the evidence being put forth right now isn't all that important, but I guess you never know what a jury's going to latch on to and there's a cumulative impact of testimony."

"That's the question, isn't it? Credible eyewitness? So when does Karl testify?"

"Probably tomorrow. As near as I know, he's the prosecution's whole case. I'd like to see the show, but I suppose I'd better set my mind to making a living."

"Do you think Celeste killed Ralph?"

I had asked myself that question a thousand times since Ralph's death. "I don't know. Is she capable of it? Yes, I imagine so. But did she do it? I don't know."

"And I know Casey hasn't said anything."

"Not a word. We have an understanding that there's a brick wall between us as far as discussing the case is concerned. Discussion about any of the Wainwright matters is *verboten*. You and I know lawyers deal with that all the time, but most other folks don't understand it. That's why Casey turned down your invitation to make use of our office and library while she's in Borderview. It's hard to see, though, how she can stand camping out in Prince Albert's office, if he's around much."

Will smiled knowingly. "Since you've built this brick wall, I gather you and Casey expect to see each other now and then."

"Occasionally. I spoke with her for a few minutes after this morning's court session and prevailed upon her to join me for a late dinner at the Fremont. She has to do some trial preparation and I have a ton of work here, so I'm staying in town tonight. Mandy took the morning train to Lincoln with George and Martha and some of the Washington brood . . . including Rosemary, of course. George is dealing with a Lincoln bank on some of his financing for the Wainwright Savings stock, and they're going to stay a few days and take in the state fair."

"Speaking of the bank stock, how is the deal coming along?"

"That's one of the things we need to talk about. I told you George's condition. He's being damn stubborn about it. We're friends, but George builds a wall of his own between business and friendship. He says I can keep my finger in the law firm, but the bank has to come first. I don't think I want to be a banker the rest of my life, but this is an interesting challenge, and George has promised a good salary. You've got some say in this, Will. I made a commitment to you about a partnership, and I won't break it. Or, if you want, and I decide to be a banker, I'll just turn the practice over to you. There's nothing for me to sell or for you to buy. As Abe Lincoln said, 'a lawyer's time and advice is his stock in trade' and our reputations don't have a market value to anybody else. All you'd have to do is take over the rent on the office, and I'd take a note for what little I'd ask for the library and furnishings."

Will's brow furrowed, and his face took on a grim look. "I just don't think I want to practice alone, Ian. Some lawyers like you don't seem to be bothered by working alone, but I'd want somebody to talk things over with. I don't think I've got the disposition to be a lone wolf in this business. I won't lie to you. I really had my heart set on Ian Locke's name being on the shingle with mine."

"Could you get along with a part-time partner, at least for a while?"

"That wouldn't be a problem. As long as I can drop by the bank with a question from time to time and you can be here for some of your special clients when need be, I don't mind carrying the day to day load."

"I wouldn't try to suck up profits off of your work. I know we can come up with an equitable division of the profits if you're doing most of the work. Frankly, you'd make a hell of a lot more money your first year in practice with me only working part time."

"Being treated fairly by you isn't one of my worries, Ian."

"Okay, Will. I don't know what I'm going to do yet, but if the county court approves the bank proposal and I decide to meet George's condition, I'll keep a connection with the firm. It will be Locke and Heasty."

Will gave a sigh of relief and his face brightened noticeably. "Thank you, Ian. This eases my mind greatly. Do you think Reuben will approve the proposal?"

"It depends some on Prince Albert. I've spoken with Emily as the sole interested party under our will, and she will consent to the sale of the bank stock. She sees it as the best way of preserving what's left of her uncle's reputation, and she doesn't want a failed bank as his legacy. I'd like to have you draft a stipulation for her signature. I think you'll find one close to what we need here in the Seacrest estate file."

"I'll have it in the morning if you want to ask Emily to stop by."

"But I still have to maneuver Albert to at least a passive position on the issue. As long as his client's a potential heir, he has to be persuaded that the proposal is to her benefit . . . and that it's his idea."

"And how do you expect to do that?"

"Albert's not a total imbecile. I toss the cards on the table, show him the financial reports. And then I make it clear if the sale doesn't go through, I'll file a motion with the court to subject any other estate assets to payment of the bank obligations. I think there's a reasonable basis for personal liability against Ralph for fraud or embezzlement. Whether I have authority to do this in the absence of a third party lawsuit remains to be seen, but the remainder of the estate, one way or another, is at risk. Albert seems to believe there is additional estate, and if so, he'll want to preserve it for Celeste."

"Do you think Albert knows something we don't?"

"He might, but at this point it doesn't matter. It would take years to litigate liability issues, and by the time the lawyers were done talking, the bank would be long since buried. I'm a great believer in solving problems one bite at a time. We save the bank first . . . then we take the next bite."

"None of this is a concern if the holographic will is invalid."

"True. But that may not be known for months. We need to direct more of our effort to that issue now." I took several sheets of paper from the top of my desk and handed them to Will. I've written out some questions for Greta Kleine. I'd like to have you look them over and add to them if you see fit. I'd like to learn more about Ralph's state of mind during the period when the new will was supposedly made. I know she'll be called to testify at the trial later this week, so wait till that's over and then talk to her again. She may not realize how much she knows until we ask the right questions."

"Oh, I almost forgot." Will said. "Greta stopped by today.

Just a minute." Will got up and hurried to the outer office. Momentarily, he returned with a book in his hand. "Greta left this for you. She said that Ralph told her if anything ever happened to him, he wanted you to have this book."

I took the book and examined it. *Eight Cousins* by Louisa M. Alcott. A fine leather cover, the pages unusually worn for Ralph's library. This was a book Mandy had been looking for, but Ralph would not have known that. Louisa Alcott, for God's sake. Why would Ralph think I would covet a book by Louisa Alcott?

24

Ian

I LAY IN my bed at the Fremont, knowing that sleep would not claim me soon, because my brain was not yet ready to close down for the night. The crisp sheets were welcome though, and a pleasant breeze caressed my naked body. A flash of light burst through the window and briefly illuminated the room. *Dry lightning*, I thought. That's what farmers called the lightning storms that occasionally teased for a spell in the midst of drought and then quickly swept away, leaving only parched dust in their wake.

My mind drifted back to dinner with Casey McGlaun. It had been a quiet meal, and while I savored Casey's presence, I sensed that her thoughts had been elsewhere tonight, as were mine. Casey's mind was obviously focused on the trial that loomed again at next daybreak, and my own could not disengage from untangling the web of mysteries Ralph Wainwright had left behind. The deceased banker had unquestionably been an uninvited guest at our table. It was unfortunate, I thought, that we were constrained by the firewall we had necessarily erected between our cases, for I would have embraced Casey's insights about my case, and I would have enjoyed debating the strategies of Celeste's defense. Still, after dinner we had joked amiably about our stimulating conversation. But no sooner had I said goodnight after escorting Casey to her room than I descended into a rare melancholy. I felt very lonely as I walked to my own room at the opposite end of the second story hallway.

What was the nature of this unspoken bond I had so quickly forged with Casey? There had not been so much as a stolen kiss between us, nothing that romantically went beyond the casual offering of her hand when she had thanked me for a pleasant dinner as we parted at her doorway. Yet her touch had left me weak in the knees, giddy as a pubescent boy at first love.

I had best shake loose of the feelings, I decided. There was no future between me and this woman. In a week or so, she would step on the train and exit from my life, leaving me with nothing but a haunting memory of an enchanting friendship that might have blossomed into something more, given precious time to grow and be nurtured.

A clap of thunder rattled the building, then, another and another like cannons roaring on a raging battlefield. Spikes of lightning set the night sky on fire. The curtains billowed like phantoms from the gusts of wind that suddenly burst through the open window. I sat up in bed and reached over to lower the window some and was interrupted by a light, tentative tapping at my door.

"Who is it?" I called.

"Casey," responded a soft voice.

"Just a minute." I stumbled out of bed and made a quick, unsuccessful search for my underwear, gave up and yanked my trousers from the back of a chair and clumsily pulled them on. I opened the door and found Casey there, clad in a flimsy cotton robe.

"May I come in?" she said, her voice calm and almost businesslike.

"Of course." I stepped aside, and after she entered, I closed the door quietly behind her.

Thunder boomed again, and a flash of lightening illuminated her face revealing determined eyes. In an instant she was in my arms, her lips locked firmly to mine. I held her closely, relishing the faint scent of ambrosia, keenly aware of the firm breasts that pressed against my body, helpless to smother my arousal. Casey pulled her head back momentarily, her face tilted upward toward mine and our eyes fastened and answered all of my questions. I kissed her now, gently at first and then hungrily. My fingers traced a path from the nape of her neck, down her spine to the small of her back. Suddenly, Casey pulled away from me and stood there momentarily as if pondering a decision. She then shrugged off her robe and it slithered down her naked body and collapsed in a heap at her feet. She took my hand and led me to the bed.

I slipped out of my trousers, and in a matter of moments we coupled urgently, with a near savage frenzy, until we climbed together to the pinnacle, oblivious to the torrents of rain that poured from the black sky and splattered off the windowsill into the dusky room. Afterward, we lay silently on the bed, her body molded to mine and her head nestled against my neck as I raked her hair gently with my fingertips. Only then did I become aware of the steady pounding of the rain outside. A mortgage lifter.

I dozed off and figured an hour must have gone by when I felt Casey's lips brushing my neck before she moved onto me, and this time there was only tenderness, the two of us rocking gently like a single vessel on a placid lake.

It was still raining when I next awakened, a soft, steady rain that promised to be a soaker, one that would bring resurrection to a dead and dying prairie. It was a bit cool in the room now, and I reached for Casey but found only the warm depression left on the sheets by her body. I sat up and looked around groggily. Her robe was gone. My trousers and lost underwear were the sole occupants of the floor adjacent to the bed. She must have slipped out just moments before I woke up. For a second I wondered if it had all been a dream, but, no, Casey McGlaun had been no apparition. And what we had experienced together during our almost wordless encounter had been more than sated lust, for me anyway. This was another one of those forks in the road. Would Casey and I choose to take a path together or, at the time of decision, embark on our separate roads?

25

Ian

I WAS BACK at my office desk. I had hoped to speak with Casey before the trial resumed, but by the time I had cleaned up, shaved and dressed, she had already left her room and was, presumably, ensconced in Albert Sweeney's library for pre-trial preparation. It still chafed that she nested in that bastard's office, but I knew that propriety and ethics dictated she work there. I convinced myself it was just as well I had not caught up with her. I didn't know how she felt about last night. Perhaps it had meant nothing to her. Maybe now, in the light of day, she found herself embarrassed by the interlude. Hell, I was baffled myself as to how to handle our next meeting, so perhaps it was best that our feelings lie fallow for a while. But one way or another I would see Casey tonight.

Will knocked lightly on the door and stepped in. "Going to take in some of the trial today?"

"No," I said. "I'd better tend to business. I should talk to Prince Albert, and then I need to spend a few hours at the bank."

"I have the stipulation ready for Emily to sign. I suppose she'll be at the trial."

"Yeah, I've hardly spoken to her. She's busy pressing pen to paper during the trial. Then she's burning up the typewriter in her room at night. I guess she sends the guts of her story to the Bee by Western Union and follows up by shipping out the rest by rail. I invited her to dine with Casey and me last night, but she was too rushed."

"How was your evening with Casey?"

"Uh, nice. Very nice. She's so wrapped up in the trial we didn't get much chance to talk." That was true enough. We didn't talk much.

"The bailiff tells me Greta's going to testify this morning before they call Karl Wainwright. I thought I might sit in on her testimony. Maybe it would help to have a friend there."

"That's a good idea. While you're over there, why don't you try to get Emily to sign the stipulation? I wouldn't think Greta's testimony would take that long. She's not an eyewitness."

"I suppose Jess is trying to shore up motive. Greta sure enough gave Celeste motives to feel like killing Ralph."

Will left and I remained at my desk working on a land contract that demanded my attention. The rain started hammering on the roof above me and I looked out the window to see sheets of driving rain. The streets were already turning to mush, and with the gully washer that was coming down now, the town square would be a lake by afternoon. And the corn would grow, and the pastures would green-up, and the cattle would fatten, and the merchants would sell, and the borrowers would pay their loans at the bank.

I put my handwritten draft of the contract aside. I'd get Will to type it later. It occurred to me that after Will was admitted to the bar, I couldn't expect him to do my clerical chores any longer.

He would have his own projects, and it wouldn't be an efficient use of his time anyway. I supposed we would have to employ a secretary or clerk. I wondered about Will's belle, Elizabeth. Will had remarked once that she was faster on the typewriter keys than he. Women were finding their ways into some of the city law offices now as clerks and secretaries. I made a note to ask Will about it.

Ralph's gift, *Eight Cousins*, still rested on my desktop, and I picked it up. I couldn't imagine what Ralph was thinking. He knew I envied his fabulous library, and while I thought Louisa M. Alcott maneuvered the English language through a story quite well, her novels were never particularly engrossing to me. Also, Ralph was never a particularly thoughtful person, and it seemed out of character for him to be thinking about doing something kind for Ian Locke upon his demise. I started thumbing through the pages, which, I had noted earlier, were surprisingly well worn. Was Ralph a surreptitious reader? At page 84, noting a crimped corner, I stopped. In the left margin, subscribed in thick, black ink appeared the initials "R.W." I studied the adjacent text, and then moved on through the book, before returning to page 84. This page seemed to have drawn Ralph's attention.

It was the second page of chapter eight of the novel, so I began reading at the beginning of the chapter. The scene was set in the library of a home where a girl named Rose seemed to be reviewing a list of books with her Uncle Alec. There is evidently some issue about Rose's handwriting, as Uncle Alec peruses the book list and asks, "Is that meant for *Pulverized Bones* ma'am?" Rose replies, "No, sir; it's *Paradise Lost*." And next to Rose's reply appear Ralph Wainwright's initials.

I set the book aside and penned a note to Will to draft a motion for a court order to allow the special administrator to enter the Wainwright house owned by Celeste for the purpose of identifying assets that might constitute property of Ralph's estate. I was seeking particular assets, but to say more might tip our hand and abort the search.

26

Casey

HALF A DOZEN buckets made annoying music as they caught the water that dripped from the ceiling of Borderview's new town hall. The roof had been previously untested and now failed in its first battle against the elements. It was a miserable day, Casey thought, but the cheerful faces among the spectators granted an almost unanimous verdict in favor of the rain. Casey smiled to herself. She had to concede that the storm had brought its personal compensations.

Greta Kleine's morning testimony had inflicted no mortal wounds to the defense. Casey had taken a pass on cross-examining Greta. She was obviously a sympathetic creature to the male jury. Who could argue that Celeste did not have good cause to be angry and bitter at Ralph's indiscretions, especially one that had resulted in an impregnated paramour? Most of the jurors were married men who knew how their own wives might respond to such circumstances. Casey was not about to argue lack of motive, and a handwritten copy of the holographic will authenticated by the clerk of the county court was submitted without defense objection by the prosecution. The validity of the will was irrelevant. It clearly established motive. Ralph Wainwright's death was in Celeste's apparent financial interest. It all came down to one question: did she do it? The way Casey saw it, the outcome hinged on Karl Wainwright's testimony.

Celeste was again seated next to Casey. This morning she had appeared bored with the entire proceedings, yawning frequently as some of the testimony grew tedious, rolling her eyes at witness responses she found ludicrous. Casey had chastened her to at least pretend being interested and sincere and to avoid theatrics that might offend, but she was not certain her words had not fallen on deaf ears. They had argued quietly but heatedly over Celeste's announcement she would like to testify in her own defense. Casey had bluntly told Celeste she would be a fool to do so but placated her by promising to discuss it before she presented the defense case.

Casey expected Karl Wainwright's testimony to take most of the afternoon. She felt inadequately prepared for the witness, who had successfully evaded her efforts to locate and interview him. Sheriff Isaac Bell and Jess Cooper had told her Karl was an eyewitness and little more. She turned to Celeste and asked, "Again, is there anything at all I should know about this man? Any reason why he would contrive a story?"

Celeste smiled benignly. "Honey, I've told you everything I know. This man's mouth opens and a lie pops out. Ralph always said that lying was just a habit with Karl. Even if the truth was in his favor, he'd rather fib his way out of trouble than tell the truth. He's a goddamn snake . . . that's what he is."

The jury members had taken their seats for the afternoon session now, and momentarily Judge Hutchens limped to his station and reconvened the court. "Mr. Cooper," he said, "let's head this train up the tracks. Call your next witness."

"Yes, your Honor. The state calls Mr. Karl Wainwright."

A slight, almost skeletal, man emerged from the crowd of spectators and made his way to the witness chair. Karl Wainwright was a pale man, with white-blond hair and feral, washed-out blue eyes, who reminded Casey of an emaciated, albino mountain lion she had seen when she lived among the Comanche. As he sat down, Wainwright's long, effeminate fingers smoothed a thin moustache that was nearly invisible from the defense table. He was dressed impeccably in a fashionable black suit and string tie.

Jess Cooper commenced his examination of Karl Wainwright, spending unnecessary time, Casey thought, on the preliminaries, but it gave her a chance to size up the witness. She concluded this was a man who was serenely confident and, who, despite a voice with an irritating nasal quality, was well spoken and probably not easily derailed from whatever story he had to tell.

Finally, Cooper cut into the meat of Wainwright's testimony. "Mr. Wainwright, were you a frequent visitor in the home of your father and stepmother?"

"A point of clarification, sir. The defendant is not my stepmother. Her name . . . as near as I know . . . is Celeste Kimball. She was never married to my father."

Celeste's marital status had been brought out in early testimony, but Karl had been quick to respond to Cooper's subtle prompt to remind the jury this was not a chaste and Christian woman upon whom they were rendering judgment.

Wainwright continued. "But to respond more directly to your question: I was not a frequent visitor to the home. Miss Kimball had made it very clear after she took up residence with my father that my presence was not welcome."

"Did she say why?"

"Objection, your Honor. Irrelevant," Casey interjected.

"Sustained. You'll need to lay more foundation if you wish to pursue that issue, Mr. Cooper."

Cooper proceeded with his examination. "Mr. Wainwright, you testified earlier that you have resided in Kansas City for the past several years. How often did you see your father during that time?"

"Perhaps twice a year. When he made business trips to Kansas City."

"And when was his most recent visit?"

"About a month before his death."

"Did he say anything at the time of that final visit that gave you concern about his well being?"

"Yes, sir, he did."

"And what did he say?"

"He said he feared for his life."

"And did he say why?"

"Yes. He said that Miss Kimball had threatened to kill him. He was afraid she would poison him, and he said he wanted me to know in case of his unexpected death under suspicious circumstances. His statement left me very concerned."

The jurors leaned forward, almost as one, to give the witness their undivided attention. Casey studied Wainwright's face. She saw no sign of nervousness. His eyes betrayed nothing. His testimony was calm, matter of fact, as though he were observer, not participant, in the events he related.

"Did your father say why the defendant threatened to kill

him?"

"Yes. He told me in a very summary way about his relationship with the maid, Miss Kleine. He said Miss Kimball had found out about the liaison and had told him he would be dead before he left her for another woman."

"You said you were concerned about your father. Did you act upon those concerns?"

"Yes, sir. A week before my father's death I returned to Borderview."

"To visit your father?"

"No. To see Miss Kimball."

"Why did you return to visit Miss Kimball?"

"I felt I should make her aware that I knew of her threats and that I would cause a serious investigation to be made if any ill fortune should come to my father. I did not want to embarrass my father with any perceived interference, so I determined I would not make him aware of my presence until I had more or less settled the issues with Miss Kimball."

"And did you speak with Miss Kimball?"

"Yes, I did, on two occasions."

"And where did this take place?"

"At the home. I went there while my father was at work."

"Did you confront Miss Kimball?"

"Yes. The first time was the Tuesday afternoon prior to my father's death."

"And what happened on that occasion?"

"We met in the library and I told Miss Kimball that I knew about her threats. I warned her that she would not get away with it if any harm came to my father."

"What was her response?"

"She just laughed and insisted she had made no such threats . . . that my father had been drinking heavily and was hallucinating. She urged me to return on Thursday, however, to discuss what she called 'mutual concerns' about my father's condition."

"Did you comply with her request?"

"Yes, I went to the house again on Thursday afternoon."

"What happened on that occasion?"

"Miss Kimball made a proposition."

Cooper was silent for a few moments, heightening the suspense. "What was the nature of the proposition?"

"She proposed we form an alliance for the murder of my father. She said there was a will that left all of my father's estate to her, but she feared he would change it and leave everything to Greta Kleine and 'her bastard,' as she put it. She said she would divide the estate with me in equal shares if I would kill my father."

"How did she propose to murder your father?"

"She said we could make it look like an accident. She would lure him into a drinking binge and then I was to kill him with a hammer or other such implement, and we would make it appear he had fallen down the stairway in a drunken stupor."

"What was your response to this proposal?"

Wainwright showed no emotion. "I told her she was insane and that I would have no part of it. I warned her I would go to my father if she persisted in such talk. She responded with profanities I would rather not repeat. Our conversation lasted no more than fifteen minutes that day. I left when I saw her outrage allowed no rational discussion."

"Did you see Miss Kimball again that week?"

"Yes, I did. The night of my father's death."

"Would you describe the circumstances."

"Yes, of course. It was Saturday evening. Dusk was just coming on. Miss Kimball's proposal had been weighing heavily on my mind, and I determined that I must make my father aware that his worst fears . . . which I had to that point doubted . . . were undeniably justified. I went to the home to alert him to the danger and to persuade him that he must cut all connections to this woman, vacate the house immediately, if necessary."

"You are referring to your father's house?"

"Well, Miss Kimball's house, actually. At least she had so informed me on my first visit. He had succumbed to her pressure to deed the house to her."

"Objection, your Honor," Casey snapped. "The witness is testifying as to facts which are not within his knowledge. His reply includes elements of speculation prejudicial to the defendant."

The judge nodded in agreement. "Sustained. The jury will disregard the reference to the deceased's motivation for deeding the residence to the defendant."

Casey knew that the judge's admonition was to no avail, but the occasional objection might force opposing counsel and witness to tiptoe more carefully around such testimony. The outcome of her case did not hinge upon this particular statement.

The county attorney continued. "Mr. Wainwright, please tell the jury what happened when you arrived at the house."

"Well, when I arrived, I knocked at the door, but there was no answer. Then it occurred to me the maid was probably off for the day. My father usually granted his servants a day's respite on Saturdays. So I checked the door, found it unlocked and entered the house."

"Then what happened?'

"I heard movement in the kitchen, so I walked down the hallway in that direction. When I reached the doorway, I saw my father sitting there with his head drooped on the kitchen table. The defendant was standing behind him holding a pistol aimed at the back of his head. Before I could say a word, the gun fired. I can remember blood spreading across the table, the smell of gunpowder and a terrible ringing in my ears. I am not proud to say I turned and ran from the house."

"Did the defendant see you there?"

"She gave no indication of it. I left quietly, not wanting to draw her fire."

"Can you describe the weapon?"

"It was an Army Colt revolver. My father kept one in his library desk, one he brought home from the war. I assume it was his . . . but I don't know."

Casey had not intended to interpose an objection over Wainwright's conjecture, but he had obviously anticipated one. This man was a witness to be reckoned with. The ownership of the weapon was not the essential issue here, but she made a mental note to ask Celeste what she knew concerning the whereabouts of Ralph Wainwright's revolver.

Cooper asked, "You said your father's head was 'drooped' on the kitchen table when you first saw him. Would you explain what you meant by that? Was he unconscious?"

"That was my impression. He was not moving."

"Did you see any blood or other evidence of violence before the gun fired."

"No, he might have been sleeping, for all I could tell."

"So, the defendant shot him in cold blood."

Before Wainwright could respond, Casey leaped to her feet. "Objection, your Honor. Counsel is not only leading the witness, he is doing so with inflammatory words."

"Sustained. The jury will disregard." Judge Hutchens looked sternly at the county attorney. "Consider yourself duly warned, Mr. Cooper."

"Yes, your Honor." Cooper turned back to his witness. "Now, Mr. Wainwright, I would like to go back over these events with you in more detail."

The county attorney spent the next hour laying the bricks of Karl Wainwright's testimony like a stonemason, filling in the chinks and cracks, smoothing out the words with care as he built the foundation of his case. Casey gave Cooper his due. He was making effective use of a witness who appeared quite credible, and who thus far had been unflappable.

When Cooper was finished with Wainwright's examination, the judge asked, "Miss McGlaun, I assume you will have a question or two of the witness?"

"Yes, your Honor, I expect to spend some time with this witness."

"Very well. We'll take a fifteen minute recess." The judge moved as quickly out of the building as his gimpy leg would permit and headed for the privy behind the building that Deputy Jimmy Hawkins would guard like a military outpost against all invaders until the judge had finished his mission and tried to emerge with some remnant of judicial dignity intact.

While Casey waited for court to reconvene, she reviewed Karl Wainwright's testimony with Celeste. "Is there anything I should know, Celeste? Karl's cross-examination could decide the outcome of your case."

"I told you before. He's a weasel. He's concocted this whole story. He approached me about killing Ralph. He couldn't have known about the holographic will until it was filed for probate. I never told him about it. He probably assumed he would get Ralph's estate. He was the only child. Ralph had been sending him money for one wild scheme after another ever since he left Borderview."

"Why would Karl kill Ralph if he depended on him for funds?"

"Because Ralph was going to cut him off. That's what they talked about on Ralph's last trip to Kansas City. That's what Ralph told me anyway. He said Karl threw one of his tantrums. He's not always the iceman you've seen today. When he doesn't get his way, he goes absolutely berserk. He might do anything in one of his rages. That's probably what happened when he killed that little girl."

Casey had heard the story from Emily Stanton. Emily had not been inclined to shrug off the tale as rumor. "Do you know he raped and killed the girl?"

"Can I prove it? No. But Ralph and I both knew. Ralph wasn't blind, even to his flesh and blood. He saw Karl's twisted side. Once, when he was drunk, he told me about Karl's cruelties as a boy . . . how one time he poured lamp oil on a cat and set it on fire, how he tortured frogs and mice by cutting off their legs while they still lived. When he was seventeen, he buggered a twelve-year old stable boy, and Ralph had to pay off the parents to stave off the law. He was always in some kind of trouble when he was away at school, and when Karl couldn't lie out of it, Ralph had to pay. But Ralph was going to yank away the money tit."

"So, you are telling me you think Karl killed Ralph?"

"I don't know who killed Ralph. But it wasn't me. I'd put Karl at the top of the list."

"What about the gun? Did Ralph have an Army Colt?"

"Yes. But it wasn't to be found when Ike Bell showed up with his warrant. I don't know what became of it. I haven't seen the weapon but once, when Ralph opened the locked drawer to get some legal papers out a year or so ago. It could have been gone a long time for all I know. Karl certainly knew about the gun, though, didn't he?"

Casey digested what Celeste had told her. She did not know whether Celeste had committed the murder, and it did not matter. She was dutybound to defend the woman to the best of her ability. The prosecution was short of hard evidence, but so was the defense. Karl Wainwright had motive to commit the murder, and, accordingly, ample motive to lie. He was Casey's best bet to squeeze out some reasonable doubt in favor of her client.

After the judge returned and called the courtroom to order, Casey stood and commenced her cross-examination of Karl Wainwright. Their eyes locked and he did not flinch, but she could see the sparks of his contempt there. "Mr. Wainwright, you have testified that you are familiar with the contents of a certain holographic will which names Celeste Kimball as the recipient of your father's estate . . . a will which has been admitted as evidence in this proceeding. Is that correct?"

"Yes, ma'am."

"Have you consulted with an attorney about the legal effect of this will?"

The county attorney stood, shaking his head in feigned

disbelief. "Objection, your Honor. Irrelevant. The terms of the will are clear. This witness's testimony on that question has no bearing on the defendant's guilt or innocence."

The judge looked at Casey, granting her a chance to reply.

"Your Honor, if the court will be patient for a few moments, I will be able to show relevance, not only as to the credibility of this witness but as to the fact that the defendant is not the only person with motive to murder Ralph Wainwright."

A stunned silence settled on the courtroom. Casey stole a glance at her anointed jurors, the blacksmith and the schoolteacher. Their attention was undivided.

"Proceed, counselor, but I'll reign you in the minute I decide this testimony's not going anywhere."

"Thank you, Judge." Casey turned back to her witness. "Mr. Wainwright, do you want me to repeat my question?"

"No, ma'am. I did consult with a lawyer."

"Good. Then I would ask you to indulge me a moment and hypothesize with me. Just for the sake of argument, assume that the holographic will is admitted to probate. Assume further that the defendant is convicted of the murder of your father. Who would inherit his estate?"

Wainwright looked bored. "His next of kin."

Karl was being just a little too clever, unnecessarily evasive when it served no point. "And who might that be?"

"Me, I guess."

"You guess?"

"I was advised that a murderer . . . in this case a murderess . . . cannot benefit from the death of a victim, so any provision in the will for Miss Kimball would be invalid."

"So, in fact, it is conceivably in your financial interest that the defendant be found guilty of murder?"

"You could say that. But it's ridiculous to suggest I might do any harm to my father."

"We'll let the jury decide what's ridiculous and what isn't, Mr. Wainwright. I'd like to go back to the Saturday night in question and go over a few points I don't quite understand. First, when you went to the house, you testified that you knocked at the door, but no one answered. How would you characterize your knock at the door?"

"What do you mean?"

"For instance, was it a hard knock or a soft knock?"

Wainwright's brow furrowed. "I don't know. It was just a knock."

"Did you knock more than once? For instance, when no one answered the first time, did you try again?"

Wainwright shrugged. "I suppose so . . . yes."

"And would it be fair to assume that knock would have been louder?"

"Objection, your Honor," said the county attorney. "This is irrelevant."

The judge did not wait for rebuttal from Casey. "This is the prosecution's witness, Mr. Cooper, and defense counsel is entitled to some latitude in cross. And the witness testified previously about his entry on the premises, so I think Miss McGlaun can pursue that line of inquiry for the moment at least."

Casey stepped closer to the witness. "I don't wish to belabor the point, Mr. Wainwright. I'm just trying to ascertain whether you made every effort to be heard before you entered the house."

"Yes, I did. I'm sure I knocked quite loudly."

It never occurred to him it would not have been all that

unusual for a son to enter his father's house without knocking, Casey thought. That happens when the story is too well rehearsed. "Mr. Wainwright, where within your father's . . . the defendant's . . . residence is the kitchen located?"

"Off a hallway that leads from the foyer to the rear of the house."

"And when you entered, the doorway to the kitchen was open. And you testified that when you came into the house, you heard movement in the kitchen. Don't you find it odd, that if you could hear movement in the kitchen that the occupant of the kitchen would not have heard you knocking?"

"I don't know. Maybe she was preoccupied."

"If you were planning to murder someone, Mr. Wainwright, don't you think you would lock the door, so you wouldn't be surprised . . . especially if the intended victim was already unconscious?"

"Objection. Calls for speculation."

"Sustained."

Casey fired back rapidly. "Mr. Wainwright. You stated you saw the defendant pointing a gun at your father. You were able to identify the make of the weapon, so you must have had a few moments to survey the situation. Why did you not yell a warning or try to stop the defendant from her alleged action?"

"I panicked. I admit it. I don't carry a weapon. I didn't believe I could do anything."

"You panicked. I guess that's understandable. So you ran for help?"

The muscles in the witness's neck tightened, and Casey could see he much preferred a friendly examiner with rehearsed responses. "No, not right away."

"Not right away. When did you contact the law, Mr. Wainwright?"

"Uh, Monday morning following the murder."

"Monday morning. A day and a half later. You say you saw your father murdered. You couldn't bring yourself to intercede at the scene, so you ran away. Could you forgive me for finding it curious that you did not go to the law until a day and a half later?"

"I suppose you might wonder."

"Would you care to explain?"

"I didn't know what to do. I was afraid Miss Kimball might try to implicate me in the killing if I admitted to being there."

"Even if you went directly to the sheriff? Does that really seem likely?"

"I suppose not. But I wasn't thinking clearly."

"Where did you go after you saw the alleged killing?"

"To the place I've been staying."

"And where might that be?"

"An old line shack on one of my father's places in Coyote Canyon . . . or it was his place. I've just learned he didn't own it anymore."

"So you were alone the night of your father's death?"

"Yes."

"You have no alibi?"

"Objection, your Honor," howled Cooper. "The witness is not on trial here."

"Your Honor, may counsel approach the bench?" Casey said.

"Yes, please do. Both of you."

The lawyers bent over the table in front of the judge, and Casey spoke in a near whisper. "Judge, I truly appreciate that the witness is not charged with the murder, but I have the right to bring forth any facts that might bear on the question of reasonable doubt. My client's life may depend upon the veracity of this witness. If there is any possibility he is perjuring himself to cast the blame for his own crime on someone else, I should be able to explore it. He is the state's case."

"Do you deny that, Mr. Cooper?" the judge asked.

"I would concede he is an important witness, yes."

"I'm going to allow Miss McGlaun to pursue this line of questioning. I don't think it's out of hand . . . yet."

Casey took her seat and posed her next question from the counsel table. "Mr. Wainwright, I know the county attorney has an aversion to speculation, but I would like to see if you might help me clarify something."

Wainwright glared at her with anger smoldering in his eyes. "You're going to ask anyway."

"How much did your father weigh?"

"I don't know. Maybe two hundred twenty pounds."

"I won't ask you how much the defendant weighs. But you wouldn't suggest she is a husky woman, would you?"

"No, of course not."

"We've heard evidence that your father's remains were discovered in a pigpen about four miles from Borderview. If the defendant murdered your father, how do you suppose she could have moved the body from the house to the pigpen on Tillie Fletcher's farm?"

"I haven't the slightest notion."

"Do you think she could have done this alone?" Through clenched teeth, Wainwright responded. "Of course not."

"So you are suggesting there must have been an accomplice?"

"There must have been."

"Or did you really see what you claim you saw?"

"What do you mean?"

"Did you fabricate this entire story, Mr. Wainwright?"

Wainwright's eyes began to twitch nervously. "Are you calling me a liar?"

"I'm just asking."

"I'm not lying."

Casey looked meaningfully at the jurors. "That will be for the jury to decide," she said. She thought she read some uncertainty in the eyes of the teacher and the smithy.

Remaining seated, Casey said, "I have just a few more questions, and I'll let you go. Is it true, Mr. Wainwright, that over the past five years or so you received substantial amounts of money from your father?"

Wainwright looked to Cooper for help, but found none. "He made investments with me from time to time."

"Now, Mr. Wainwright, please understand that if you prefer I can have you called as a hostile witness for the defense, after testimony by Mr. Arnold Tilson, who has completed an audit of your father's accounts. But we can dispose of this very quickly if you will answer my questions forthrightly. With that in mind, would it be fair to say that your father advanced you in excess of $75,000 over the past five years?"

"It's possible. We were investing heavily in Kansas City real estate."

"I see. And did he ever receive any return on his investments? Was any of the money ever paid back?"

"They were long-term investments. There has been no return yet."

Casey decided to let the jurors draw their own conclusions. She could sense the judge's impatience and knew she was a question or two away from being shut down. "A final question. Is it true that your father had recently informed you he would be making no further advances . . . or perhaps we should call them investments?"

"Objection," yelled the county attorney, leaping from his seat.

"I withdraw the question," said Casey. "The defense has no further questions of this witness."

27

Ian

THE COUNTY JUDGE did not hesitate to sign an order authorizing me to enter the Wainwright house for an asset search. Unfortunately, Albert Sweeney had prevailed in his demand that the search be carried out in his presence and that of Sheriff Isaac Bell, both of whom were currently ranked near the top of my list of horse's asses.

Will Heasty and I stood in the shade of an oak tree outside the mansion waiting for Ike Bell and Prince Albert to show up with the key. The sun had popped out this morning after another nightlong drencher, but dark, rolling clouds in the west suggested that by nightfall buckets would be pouring from the heavens again. There never seemed to be an in-between in Nebraska. We tended to go from drought to flood and back to drought again. At least that's the way it appeared to those folks who made their ways through life trying to grub a living from the soil.

I was in a foul mood this morning, and it was Casey McGlaun's fault the way I saw it. I had been unable to rendezvous with her after the trial recessed yesterday. I had worked at the bank until suppertime and then returned to The

Fremont to find Casey. I encountered Emily in the dining room, and she informed me that Casey had taken a sandwich to Sweeney's office and was preparing for the next day's court session. At Emily's invitation, I joined her for some vegetable stew and sourdough bread and got an update on the trial's progress. I learned that the prosecution had rested its case and Casey would commence presentation of her defense this morning. Casey had asked Judge Hutchens to allow two days for the defense's evidence, and the case was expected to go to the jury by Friday.

After supper I went to the law office and cranked out some paperwork. I call it "supper" when I have soup in the evening. It's "dinner" if I have steak. Sometimes I have "dinner" at noon, but on other occasions I have "lunch." If I eat at home, the evening meal is always supper and the noon meal is always dinner. People newly arrived from the east are often confused by the way we country folk label our meals, but those of us who have lived here a few years have no trouble with the nuances. We know exactly when we're eating lunch, dinner or supper. Anyway, I had returned to The Fremont about nine o'clock and rapped on Casey's door, but she had evidently not returned. I tried again to no avail an hour later and gave up. I didn't sleep worth a damn last night, unable to get my mind off of this wild spirit-creature who called herself Casey McGlaun, and it didn't help that she was not in her room when I checked to see if we might meet up for breakfast. Mandy was returning this afternoon from her state fair excursion with George and his kids, and although I was anxious to see her, I knew it meant a return to nights at the ranch, and I began to wonder if I would ever get a glimpse of the red-headed barrister again.

"You seem a mite preoccupied, Ian," Will said, tugging me from my reverie.

"My mind's straying some," I admitted. "Some days I'm not of this earth and this is one of them, I guess."

Will nodded toward the hitching rail where our horses were tied. "Better come home for a spell. Ike and Prince Albert are here."

Sweeney, as Celeste's attorney, had custody of the key, and after an exchange of cool greetings, he let us in the house. Will and I slipped off our muddy boots in the foyer, and Ike looked at us like we were addled. "Celeste says there's nothing here," said Sweeney. "Ralph kept all of his financial papers at the bank. But we can look around. Where do you want to start?"

"With the books."

"With the books? You're not going to inventory the goddamned books? That'll take days. Hell, I don't even know if they belong to the estate. Celeste owns the house. I'd say the contents go with it."

"That's not necessarily true, Albert, and you know it. It's all a matter of intent. If the estate can establish Ralph paid for the books, and Celeste doesn't have a bill of sale from him, I'd say the estate owns the books." I winked at Will. "Wouldn't you say so, Will?"

"I'd say so. I'm sure there's some case law on that point."

There was only one book I cared anything about, but I always took a sadistic pleasure in baiting Albert. "Let's get started," I said, leading the way to the library.

Ike Bell plopped down in a chair at the library table and ran his crocodilian eyes over the book-lined walls. I doubted if he had ever seen half that many books in one place before. It was a safe bet he had not read a book in his lifetime. "Jesus Christ," Ike said. "What in the hell does a man do with so many books?"

Will ran his fingers reverently along the spines of the perfect covers. "I'm envious, Ian. This is an unbelievable collection. I had no idea Ralph had such a library."

Sweeney whined, "You're wasting your time, Locke. These books would bring a nice price in a big city. I can't advise Celeste to walk away from her claim to the library."

"Hell, Albert, you're trying to probate a will that leaves everything to Celeste. If you're successful, she ends up with the books anyway. Worried about your case?"

A sneer crossed his lips. "Not in the slightest. I just expect you to leave the books out of the inventory."

"Will," I said, "why don't you take the east wall and I'll take the west?"

Sweeney's brow furrowed as Will and I examined the book titles while we moved slowly along the floor-to-ceiling oak bookcases. "Are you going to make a list?" Sweeney asked.

I didn't respond. Momentarily, I spotted the book and removed it from the shelf. It was a tall book with an elegant leather cover. I opened it and found what I was looking for instantly. Spread across the front inside cover was a final message from Ralph Wainwright. I sat down at the table and Will joined me.

I held up the closed book. "John Milton's *Paradise Lost* and Ralph's last will."

"What in the hell are you talking about?" Sweeney asked, a look of total puzzlement on his face.

"Ralph wrote another will on the inside cover of the book. God knows I recognize his handwriting after these past few weeks. Bear with me while I read."

I looked at Sweeney and the sheriff and saw I had their undivided attention. I began to read slowly to properly dramatize my discovery:

"This is my last will. I wrote out another will three days ago. I did this while Celeste Wainwright, who is really Celeste Kimball, stood beside me. I made out that will because I was being blackmailed. If I die, I don't want that will to stand, and I hereby cancel it. I want the will I did with Ian Locke to be my will, and I want my niece, Emily Stanton, to get all of my property. I still name Ian Locke as executor. I get the last word, Celeste. Signed by me on June 4, 1884. Ralph Wainwright."

Sweeney slammed his fist on the table. His face had turned crimson, and I could almost see smoke blowing from his ears. "Locke, you son of a bitch, what kind of bullshit is this? Let me see that book."

I handed him the book and waited silently while he examined Ralph's message. After a few minutes he slid the book back down the table. "This is pure shit. How did you know about this? How do I know you didn't write it?"

"Albert, in open court I'll tell you how I found out about it. For the moment, let's just say Ralph told me. As for my writing it, you know that's Ralph's handwriting, but either way it can be proven the same way you were going to prove the other holographic."

"You can't have a will written inside a book cover," the sheriff remarked after watching the proceedings in stony silence. He looked at Sweeney. "Can you, Albert?"

Sweeney ignored the sheriff's question. A mask of sweetness now covered his face. "Well, Ian, I don't think you have much there, but in the interest of getting this resolved, I'd be willing to convey a settlement proposal to Celeste."

"We've got nothing to talk about, Albert. Either your will is invalid because it was signed under duress, in which case the earlier will was never revoked . . . or this will is a new holographic will that cancels the previous holographic will. Either way, you and Celeste lose."

"We'll see about that," Sweeney blustered.

I handed the book to Will. "We've all seen what's in this book, so we're taking it with us. We'll be filing it in the county court with proper pleadings tomorrow."

"I don't think so, Ian," said Ike Bell, his chest swelling like a proud rooster's. "I'm the law here. I'm going to take custody of this evidence."

"You don't have the authority, Ike. If the judge ordered you to be here, show me the signed writ. I assume you came at Albert's request, and I've got to tell you this troubles me some. It makes me wonder about Albert's judgment."

Bell bristled. "Just what in the hell do you mean by that?"

"Ralph wrote that he was blackmailed into making the second will. I've had an audit made at the bank, and I'm wondering if he was paying off another blackmailer."

The sheriff said nothing. Sweeney, visibly irritated since this session at the Wainwright house had delivered nothing but bad news, said, "What are you getting at Locke? I don't see what this has got to do about anything."

I ignored Sweeney's remark and bore in on Ike Bell. "Ike, the auditor advised me you had received over $10,000 in checks from Ralph over the past five years, and there's a $2,000 note with the bank he never tried to collect on. I figure that's about three times the salary you've gotten from the county over the same period of time. I'd say that's damn serious money. Can you explain what you did that was worth so much?"

Bell's eyes darted nervously and beads of sweat broke out on his forehead. "I . . . I did security work for Ralph . . . at the bank and here at the house."

"Security work? Like what?"

Sweeney suddenly had an interest in the conversation now. "Yeah, Ike, like what?"

"Well, like I kept a special lookout at the bank at nights just to be sure there wasn't nobody trying to break in. And I gave him advice about what to do if there was a robbery . . . all kinds of things. Then Ralph worried a fearsome amount about Celeste being took for ransom, so I kept an eye out for anybody hanging out around here . . . strangers and such."

Sweeney remarked, "Hell, Ike, that's what we pay tax dollars for. And the sheriff doesn't have off duty time. I seriously question the ethics, if not the legality, of your taking money for those services. Regardless, Ralph could have hired a couple of guards around the clock for what you got paid. I truly don't understand this."

The sheriff was squirming now, ready to call it a night. He had lost interest in taking custody of the book. "Nobody's business what Ralph was paying me for."

"It is if you were blackmailing him," I said. "Ralph got the bank in financial trouble, and as special administrator of his estate, I have a responsibility to follow the money and recover whatever I can. You see, Ike, I've got a theory. Would you like to hear it?"

"Hell, no. Your theories ain't worth a four card flush." Bell pushed his chair back and started to get up.

Will Heasty finally spoke. "Wait a minute, Ike. This is news to me, too. I'd like to hear Ian's theory."

Bell was obviously torn between his curiosity and his desire to absent himself from this place. Curiosity won out and he stayed put. "All right, show your cards."

"Here's what I think, Ike. I'm pretty sure this goes back to the rape and murder of that poor little girl outside the carnival grounds over five years ago. I think you came across some evidence that Karl Wainwright did it and you went to Ralph with the information. You made a deal that Karl would leave town and carry out his rapes and killings in some other community, and as long as Ralph kept the checks coming you'd keep your mouth shut. I've seen despicable acts in my time but none any lower. Not only a guilty man went unpunished, but I wonder how many poor girls have died or been assaulted."

"You can't prove that. You're guessing."

"It's the truth. I can see it in your eyes. And I'm going to lay it out for the county attorney and suggest he have the state attorney general's office make a special investigation. Maybe nobody can prove anything, but you will have to do some explaining. And don't try to tell me word of the investigation won't leak out. Secrets aren't well kept in this town. If you hang on by a thread, the voters will cut you off next election day . . . if they don't lynch you before."

I paused for a moment to let my words sink into the sheriff's thick skull. His eyes would not meet my own. He looked down at the table, evidently pondering the sudden unpleasant turn of events. His face was chalk-white, and his chest was heaving like a blacksmith's bellows. I half expected him to keel over from a heart attack. Nonetheless, I continued. "One thing I can't figure out, Ike, is how you and Karl tie in to Ralph's murder. It seems too coincidental that Karl shows up, his father is killed, and he waits a few days to go to the sheriff who was blackmailing the old man to tell what he saw. The sheriff's money spigot was running dry. Maybe he figured junior would have a new one to draw from. Maybe junior and the sheriff teamed up."

"That's exactly what happened," Sweeney said enthusiastically. "Ike and Karl killed Ralph."

Bell stood up, looking tired and haggard. It was like he had aged ten years since he entered the library an hour or so earlier. "All these law wranglers in here . . . this place smells like a room full of wood pussies. I've had me enough." The sheriff straightened up, sucked in his gut, and walked out of the room.

28

Ian

AFTER OUR PRODUCTIVE visit to the Wainwright mansion, Will
and I returned to the office with our discovery. We sat down in
my office to discuss the turn of events and to plot our course.
Outside, the sky was turning smoky gray and clouds were
churning angrily. The low rumble of thunder could be heard in
the southwest, and I fretted over prospects of a stormy ride to the
ranch after I met Mandy at the depot this afternoon. Of course, I
could rent another room at The Fremont and we could stay in
town overnight. And after Mandy was asleep, I could call on
Casey and pray for another thunderstorm if that's what it took to
get her back in my arms. Somehow, Casey McGlaun was not
bringing out my nobler motives this day.

Will was sitting next to my desk, studying the thick, black
words inscribed on the inside cover of *Paradise Lost* for perhaps
the tenth time, shaking his head in disbelief. "It's too easy," he
said. "We're supposed to win our cases with superior skills and
brains, aren't we? This just fell in our laps."

"I'll take dumb luck over brains most of the time. That's the
way it works in this business, Will. We stumble on a bit of

information solely by accident or our mind plucks an idea from nowhere. Suddenly, we look a hell of a lot smarter than we are. Anymore, I let the client attribute that piece of luck to my genius, because I know my skill and brilliance will go totally unrecognized when things go sour because of the other lawyer's dumb luck or because the judge's breakfast didn't set well or his wife didn't share his ardor the night before."

"How could Ralph have been certain you would find his clue in *Eight Cousins*? How did he figure it out in the first place? I never thought of Ralph as literary. I don't know why he just didn't write out a new will or let you know what had happened."

"Like most of us, Ralph did his share of stupid things . . . maybe more than his share . . . but he was a man of substance once, and it wasn't all by accident. He wasn't the smartest man in this part of the country by any means, but he had an innate cunning that enabled him to outfox more bookish men. I suspect he figured out his clue by happenstance. Almost everyone's at least heard of Louisa Alcott. He probably pulled *Eight Cousins* from the shelf and randomly thumbed through it and came on the words *Paradise Lost*, a title a lot of folks might recognize even if they hadn't read it. From the looks of it, someone had read *Eight Cousins*, possibly several times before. Maybe he was familiar with it. Anyway, something triggered the idea to use the book. I think he was a virtual prisoner in the home during those last days. We know that Prince Albert and Celeste were searching all the papers in the house. They probably wanted to be sure Ralph hadn't left something like this behind. Even if they searched the library, they wouldn't have done more than look for loose papers."

"That's true. They couldn't thumb through the pages of every book. They couldn't begin to."

"He could hardly talk to me without discussing the blackmail that had forced him into making out the earlier holographic will, and I don't think he wanted that discovered while he was still alive. That's why he didn't just write something out on paper and give it to Greta. It could have fallen into someone else's hands. If he and Greta had a falling out, Ralph might have had trouble recovering the document. A Louisa Alcott book would have had no significance to anyone. The only reason it had any meaning to me was the curiosity it raised when Greta delivered it."

"He took a big chance."

"Yes, it was risky. But he probably realized that a book was about the safest thing in that house. But what if we hadn't picked up on the clue? By this time, Ralph had to know he was close to broke. My guess is that he had already informed Karl that the checks were coming to a stop. That's probably what really brought him back to Borderview. He wouldn't have believed the old man was out of money even if Ralph told him. People like that have to be hit over the head with the truth. Ike might have got the same message and forged a new alliance with Karl as soon as he could."

"So do you think Karl or Ike had something to do with Ralph's death?"

I shrugged. "Anything's possible."

"I assume we should go ahead and get our new will on file with the county court today."

"Yes, go ahead and type up a copy for our file and then we'll both sign a verification that it's the exact wording of the holographic version . . . just in case the book mysteriously disappears. I'm not inclined to leave anything to chance."

"Are we going to try to probate this one or just submit it as evidence that the first one was never revoked?"

"Obviously, Reuben's never dealt with anything quite like this . . . neither have I, for that matter. I think I'll draft an alternative pleading and let him take his pick. It would probably be cleaner to probate our first will, though, and when we have the hearing, I'll try to nudge him in that direction. I'm going to file a motion that the hearing be set next week for admitting the will to probate. Celeste's trial is about over, and the new will makes that a moot issue anyway. As soon as I'm appointed executor, we can go ahead with the bank arrangements. Emily's in full accord and she calls the shots on the estate's financial dealings from here on. I just hope we can salvage something for her out of this mess. She feels a responsibility to do something for Greta and the baby."

I heard the door open in the outer office. Will got up to see who had come in and returned momentarily with a Western Union in his hand. He handed it to me and I opened it and scanned the words quickly. "It's from my brother, Cam. He's arriving on tomorrow afternoon's train. Doesn't say why."

29

Ian

DUSK DESCENDED AS Mandy and I rode into the Lazy Key ranch yard. A storm still threatened but it had held off long enough to leave me without an excuse to stay in town. A buggy would never have made it through the murk and mire of our county roads, so I rented a horse for Mandy from the livery. We had made good time, since even Hemlock had apparently sensed the need to beat bad weather home and had been a model of good behavior during the trip.

TJ was waiting on the porch when we arrived. He had evidently been visiting lady friends at Tillie Crump's when I departed for town a few days back, so he had been left to his own devices in my absence. I smiled to myself, thinking TJ and I both had our weaknesses when it came to the female sex. Wolf was nowhere in sight. I hoped he had not taken up TJ's wandering ways. George had offered to castrate the dog to encourage him to stay close to home, but I held empathy for the animal that pushed me toward reprieve. Wolf was a hunter, and the local jackrabbit population kept him largely self-sufficient, but one of George's older sons checked the place daily and was to drop off some rancid beef from time to time to supplement the dog's diet.

As we dismounted, Mandy said, "Dad, I want to see Dancer. I'll put up the horses if you want to get supper started."

"You sure?"

She looked at me in feigned exasperation. "Dad, not everybody hates horses."

"I don't hate horses. I swear I don't. They just don't like me. And it's mostly Hemlock that gives me trouble."

"I'm sorry, Dad. It's nothing to be ashamed of. But they sense it. Deep down you just do not like horses."

We had shared this conversation before, so I held up my hands in mock surrender. "Okay, you unsaddle and grain the horses. I'll see what I can scratch up for supper. You'll probably have to settle for biscuits and beans. Maybe we can do some ginger cookies together after supper."

Mandy was already on her way to the barn with Hemlock and the rented mare in tow. TJ followed behind, deserting me for his younger friend. Well, go with her, I thought. See what you find to eat in the barn. I went in the house and decided to light the oil lamp in the kitchen before darkness settled in. I started a fire in the wood stove, and then left it to burn down to red-hot coals while I changed clothes. I shucked my rumpled suit and slipped into some denim trousers and decided on a flannel shirt in light of the chill that was moving in ahead of the storm that was almost certainly signaled by ragged bolts of lightning flashing off to the southwest.

The impending storm triggered thoughts of my single night with Casey McGlaun, and as I commenced mixing up the biscuit dough and got a pot of beans started on the stovetop, I found myself dwelling once again on this woman who had somehow taken up residency in a portion of my addled brain. I'm a lawyer, and not being inclined toward the more visceral battlefields of the courtroom, I focus on bringing order out of chaos, and I tend to analyze and re-analyze to make sense out of things. I try to make logic rule my conclusions, although I confess I am often more comfortable when I allow my intuition to rule. I have learned to never entirely ignore my "gut feelings" and to at least test my carefully reasoned decisions against my more instinctive reactions. This had long been my internal strife—logic versus emotion—and I tried to give both due weight.

Logic told me there was no future for Casey and me. She had her sights set on a future that would make her the most sought after trial lawyer in the west—hell, probably the whole United States of America. That kind of career was not launched from a rural base like Cottonwood County. And I had found my piece of heaven here. The big city was not my destiny, not with Weeping Springs and Mushroom Rock a ten-minute walk from my doorstep. She was a young woman more malleable and capable of change than I, who tottered on the brink of middle age and whose mold had been pretty well cast some years back. Logic told me we had not known each other long enough to even think the thoughts I had been thinking lately. And what was on Casey's mind about the two of us?

Emotion told me, I finally conceded, that I was in love with this woman and the mere notion of losing her sent my mind spinning into near panic. The thought of Casey McGlaun made me a young man again, made me more resilient and open to change, made me ready to rethink what I might be willing to do if I had the prospect of spending a lifetime with her.

The pungent smell of overdone biscuits brought me back to

the mundane tasks at hand. As I rescued the biscuits from the oven, it occurred to me that Mandy was a bit past due from her chores in the barn. This did not especially concern me, since she had a tendency to dally with the horses, but when I went to the door and looked outside and saw how quickly the sky was darkening, I decided I needed to retrieve her immediately and hurried back into the house, grabbed up the oil lamp and headed for the barn.

When I flung back the barn's Dutch doors and stepped inside, a wave of sickening fear swept through my stomach. Neither Hemlock nor the rented mare had been unsaddled. On a backdrop of loose wheat straw just inside the doorway lay Wolf, his head and jaw mashed to shards. Blood-caked wounds in his torso indicated he had taken several bullets before being finished off with one of my long-handled axes that had been tossed aside nearby. There was no sign of Mandy. Obviously, the stalker had returned and made off with my daughter while I puttered mindlessly in the kitchen. How could I have been so careless? So utterly stupid?

I moved quickly through the barn, calling for Mandy on the chance she had found a hiding place in some nook. I checked outside the rear doors and found tracks at the exit of one, but between the darkness and the pre-rain haze, I was unable to discern anything I did not already know. My instinct was to race wildly after the tracks, but I realized my emotions were untrustworthy right now. I was weaponless in the unlikely event I caught up with Mandy's captor. If I were killed, neither Mandy nor I would be missed until sometime tomorrow, giving the abductor nearly a day's head start. The horses had not been unsaddled, so he must have taken Mandy as soon as she entered the barn, and this gave him a good hour's lead. Someone else had to be informed, and I needed help, more precisely, I needed George Washington's help.

I ran back to the house, found my slicker and an extra for Mandy, and then pulled my '73 Winchester down from the gun rack next to the door. Then, I rushed into the bedroom and opened the dresser drawer, removing the holstered Navy Colt revolver nestled there and buckled it on. I hadn't fired the pistol in some years, but I oiled and cleaned it frequently and kept the belt full of fresh cartridges. I don't like guns much, but I respect them and I know how to use them. Yes, I certainly know how to use them.

I abandoned our supper and made a beeline for the barn. I unsaddled the rented horse, tossed her some hay and left a bucket of water in her stall. Then I saddled Dancer for Mandy's return, or to be placed into service if we needed a spare mount. I apologized to Hemlock for pressing him back in to service so quickly, and for some reason he did not protest when I slid the rifle into the saddle holster and swung into the saddle. We took off for George's place just as the first volley of the storm struck.

30

Ian

GEORGE AND I took shelter under the shelf of a limestone outcropping less than a mile from his place. We got the four horses out of the weather as best we could and then pressed our backs to the rock wall and waited out the storm's onslaught. George rolled a soggy cigarette and after repeated failures finally got it lit. He stood next to me, tugging the warm smoke into his lungs, savoring it, and then exhaling it slowly in thick plumes that lingered for some moments in the heavy air before sneaking away into the sheets of rain. Somehow, I found the rich tobacco odor warming and comforting.

As luck would have it, this was the most violent gale I had ever tried to ride out. I figured we must have caught the edge of one of those angry tornadoes that sweeps over the Kansas border from time to time, twists its way through southern fringes of Nebraska wreaking havoc along its path, leaving death and destruction in its wake, before petering out and retreating like some phantom, just as quickly as it had attacked. The storms that rode with it, however, might hang on for hours.

It had taken me a half hour to make what should have been a

ten-minute trip to George's farm. With the racket of thunder and snapping lightning in the background, it had taken some serious hammering on the door to arouse a response from the house. Alexander, George's ten year-old by Willow, wife number three, had answered the door, wide-eyed and startled by the spectral appearance of the dripping figure that had emerged from the storm. I brushed past him and told him to get his father. There had been no need since George was there before the boy turned to summon him. I suspect my words sounded like gibberish, but George got the gist of my story and immediately left to collect his own weapons and stuff his saddlebags with supplies. Martha appeared momentarily and led me to a crackling fireplace in the spacious living room. A passel of small children parted like little chicks to make room in front of the fire. I savored the warmth for a few moments before George returned.

"Shall I send word to Ike?" George asked.

"Anybody but Ike. No. When the storm clears, have somebody let Will know. Tell him to give us a day. We don't need any trigger-happy drunks looking for Mandy. My brother, Cam, is arriving tomorrow afternoon. Will should tell Cam to go the Lazy Key and wait for me there. If we aren't back by nightfall tomorrow, Cam will have to calculate what to do next."

"Did you hear that, Martha?" George said.

Martha, a dark, sad-eyed woman with an aristocratic bearing, had kissed him softly on the cheek. "Yes, dear. Consider it done. Now ride with the wind. Don't come back without that precious little girl."

Willow, who looked and moved like her name, appeared just before we stepped out into the storm and tendered an oilcloth bag filled with hardtack, beef jerky and dried fruits. "God go with you," she said.

It had taken us an hour to get to this place. A mile in an hour. We knew our destination: the line shack at Coyote Canyon, at least another three miles from our shelter. It was futile to try to pick up a trail. Our first bet had to be Karl Wainwright. The second was the line shack where George had spotted him. If we didn't find Mandy or pick up a lead there, all bets were off.

I glanced at George who stood no more than three feet to my left. A flash of lightning illuminated his face, giving it a ghostly effect. His expression was grim, his obsidian eyes simmering with something almost inhuman. He cast aside the butt of his cigarette and commenced rolling another. He felt my gaze and his eyes locked with mine. I wondered if I looked as somber and menacing as my companion and decided I probably did.

George spoke in a rasping near-whisper. "A man like this will need to die. When we find him, you will leave him with me. He will touch no more children."

I shook my head. "No. Mandy is my daughter. His fate is in my hands."

"You are a man of the law. You cannot do what must be done."

I set my jaw as our eyes dueled stubbornly. "I will do what must be done."

George gave a single nod and returned his attention to fashioning the cigarette.

We stood there in silence the better part of another hour as the storm raged on. Finally, the wind began to die down and the torrents turned to mere sheets. "It's easing up," I observed.

"It will return," George said. "I know you want to get moving, but we've got to give it time to blow over . . . at least a few hours.

"A single minute could make the difference."

"Yes. And that's why we can't risk a broken leg on a horse. Or meeting up with a flash flood. Or slipping over the edge of a canyon wall. Maybe they've been slowed down, too."

"They had a good head start, and if they were headed for the canyons, they were moving east ahead of the storm."

"Don't matter. We don't have any say so over what they do. We can only control what we do."

George was right, of course. We couldn't rescue Mandy if our bodies were washed up twenty miles downriver. But the wait was agonizing. I was struck by the fact that the only comparable experiences in my life were when I suffered through two horrifying death watches as I waited for the life force to be choked out of first one young son and then the other.

As George predicted, we were not on our way in until several hours after midnight, and it was damn slow going. We fought swollen creeks, and we had to dismount and slog through mud from time to time when the murk sucked unmercifully at the hooves of our horses. It was daybreak when we forded a swollen stream that usually threaded like a slender ribbon through Coyote Canyon. The rain had finally stopped and streaks of sunlight sneaked through the downy clouds, and a splendid rainbow spanned the canyon like a heavenly archway to the south. I guessed that full sun would fight its way through the haze by midday.

We could see the faint outline of the shack in the distance, and we dismounted and tethered the horses. There was a newly revived carpet of multi-hued green grasses on the canyon floor but very little in the way of cover to protect our approach. We decided we would each work our way in from opposite sides of the canyon, hoping that Karl was not looking for pursuit just yet, if, in fact, he still occupied the little cabin. I saw no sign of a horse as I moved in closer from my angle, and this discouraged me. I feared we had placed the wrong bet when we gambled on this place. Then I reminded myself once again this had been the only bet.

When we were perhaps twenty-five yards from the shack, I signaled George to hang back while I approached the door of the cabin. If Karl took me out, Mandy would have a second chance with George. I crouched low and raced toward the cabin with my Winchester cocked and ready to fire. I expected to take a bullet at any moment, but I had determined Karl Wainwright couldn't fill me with enough lead to bring me down before I got to him and took him with me to hell. To my surprise I reached the cabin without incident, and I inched up to the shack and flattened my back against the rough pine wall and waited. Silence. Anyone inside must have been sleeping. Or must be very, very patient. I waved George in closer, and he positioned himself in the grass with his rifle sighted on the door.

Quietly, I moved along the cabin wall toward the closed door. I softly tested the door handle. The door moved without resistance. Still no response. I leaned my rifle against the cabin wall and drew my Colt revolver. Then, in a single motion, I pushed the door open and dived through, striking the floor with my left shoulder and rolling once before I swung my pistol around in search of a target. There was none. I got up and signaled George in before I looked around.

Then I spotted a rickety cot at the end of the one-room cabin, and the bile rose in my throat as I walked to it and found the signs that Karl and Mandy had been there. "Goddamned sick animal," I screamed as George came through the open doorway. "The evil, slimy bastard."

I had seen all of the horrors of war that a man could see. But this sickened me more than anything I could remember, and waves of weakness and nausea swept over me. I was only vaguely aware of George's firm hand on my shoulder as we looked at the massive splattering of recently fresh blood on the filthy feather mattress and Mandy's underpants and mud-caked denim britches in a little pile next to the cot.

31

Casey

CELESTE KIMBALL-WAINWRIGHT'S trial was going to come to an end a day early. Casey had anticipated re-calling Sheriff Isaac Bell to explore his strange connection with Karl Wainwright, but the sheriff had suddenly turned up missing. His fuzzy-faced deputy had appeared nearly tongue-tied before Judge Hutchens immediately after court convened and reported he had been unable to serve the subpoena on his superior as ordered. The sheriff had disappeared without so much as a word to anyone. Both of his horses were gone. His room at the Widow Tucker's boarding house had been cleared out, and his firearms and personal belongings had been evacuated from the sheriff's office. It was as if some ghost had spirited him away into the night.

Casey had thought long and hard about calling Celeste to testify in her own defense. Celeste, in fact, had continued to be insistent about doing so. But Casey had reservations. Celeste's story was one of simple denial. She had never plotted Ralph Wainwright's death, had never approached Karl about killing his father. The night of Ralph's death, he had left the residence on some undisclosed mission, presumably to rut with his slut on her

Saturday off. Celeste had spent the evening in the parlor reading some book, the name of which she could not recall.

There was a fair chance that Celeste would charm the male jury, but no better than fair. Smooth as she was, Casey doubted that Celeste's story could withstand rugged cross-examination. There was no way to corroborate her testimony. It was her word against Karl's. Casey felt she had established in the minds of some jurors, especially the blacksmith and the schoolmarm, that Karl was a probable liar. Intuitively, she saw Celeste as no more truthful than Karl. There were too many gaps in her tale. She professed undying love for Ralph. In spite of his philandering and his wicked ways, she could never have harmed him, or even wished for his demise. Casey doubted the woman had rarely, if ever, loved anyone as much as she loved herself. All Casey had to do was to plant a reasonable doubt in the collective mind of the jury. If she had not already accomplished that, she hoped to do so in her closing argument.

Celeste and Casey had locked horns this morning when Casey informed her client of the decision not to have her testify. "Need I remind you I am paying your fees?" Celeste had said testily.

"Not at all," Casey had replied. "Need I remind you why you are paying my fees? My job is to keep you from being the first woman to hang in Nebraska since statehood. You have the right to testify, and if you insist, I will do my best. But I promise you if there is the least bit of untruth in your testimony, the jury will see it, and you're likely to leave this earth with rope burns on that pretty neck."

Celeste had finally relented, and Casey had proceeded this morning to lay out the defense's evidence in less than an hour.

She had called as her expert witness—and only witness—Dr. Omar Hauptmann, who at her behest had examined the victim's remains and now verified it was impossible to say how Ralph Wainwright died. There had been obvious damage to the skull, but the fatal injury could have been inflicted by hammer or some other such instrument, as well as gunshot—or both. There was no apparent residue of gunpowder, although on cross-examination he conceded that Tillie Crump's hogs would likely have destroyed any such evidence.

To the obvious surprise of judge, jury and spectators, Casey, after Dr. Hauptmann's dismissal by Judge Hutchens, had softly and abruptly declared, "Defense rests."

Shortly before noon, Jess Cooper completed an impassioned closing argument on behalf of the state, extolling the victim's godlike virtues and lamenting the heinous, undignified circumstances of his death and disposal. Cooper hammered again and again at the fact there existed an eyewitness to the dastardly deed and deftly skirted other evidentiary issues. All in all, Casey thought the young prosecutor had been quite effective.

The judge declared a lunch recess, and now Casey waited to present her own closing argument while the judge conferred with the bailiff at the bench. She turned to Celeste, who looked a bit too smug. "No rolling of your eyes. Remember, you are wrongly accused. You are hurt. The jury will be watching you now. My remarks will be shorter by half than Mr. Cooper's. Be demure while I'm speaking. Sincere concern, rather than overconfidence, is best now."

"So you're not just my lawyer now. You are my acting coach as well?"

"That's right," Casey snapped. "And I'm all that stands

between you and the hangman."

"Miss McGlaun, you may proceed with closing," announced the judge.

Casey stood, pushed her notes aside and, with a thoughtful look on her face, walked slowly to the invisible jurors' box and faced the members of the jury. Her eyes locked briefly with those of the teacher and the blacksmith, the former who responded with a faint smile and blushed slightly.

"I will be considerate of your time," Casey said. "I appreciate fully that each of you is a man who is here because you have seen fit to do your duty as a citizen of this great state." She did not add that to do otherwise would subject the juror to contempt charges and possible jail time.

"I thank you for the attentiveness and courtesy you have shown throughout this trial. We have toiled together some four days . . . Judge Hutchens, the lawyers and, of course, you the jurors. In a courtroom we all work, and we hope that the end product will be justice. Very soon, when the lawyers have spoken their final words, the task will be yours alone." She paused for some moments. "You will decide if justice is done in this courtroom. It is a sobering thought, I know . . . but true." Her eyes passed over the somber jurors, pausing on the teacher whose face was unequalled in its sincerity.

"I would remind you that justice, first of all, demands that we do not punish the innocent. The protection of the innocent has the greatest priority in this system of ours, and because of that, it is fundamental in any criminal case that the defendant is not to be found guilty if there is a reasonable doubt as to his or her guilt. I am confident you understand that it is not your job to make your decision based upon probabilities. You do not find the defendant guilty if you think she *probably* committed the crime, or *may* have done it. To convict, you must be satisfied of guilt beyond any reasonable doubt. With that said, I would take just a few moments to review with you the evidence presented by the prosecution."

Casey then proceeded to discuss the testimony pertaining to cause of death and motive. She noted that several persons, given what had been revealed during the trial, could have had motives to murder Ralph Wainwright—certainly others besides Celeste. She emphasized there existed no scientific evidence to pinpoint how the victim had been killed.

"Most of the evidence in this case doesn't even approach circumstantial. It is simply non-existent. We can concede the senior Mr. Wainwright was in all likelihood murdered. There is no other reasonable explanation for his remains turning up in Mrs. Crump's pigpen. But that does not tell us who killed him, or, as I have said before, how. The 'who' and the 'how' as proposed by Mr. Cooper are dependent upon the testimony of a single witness. Please, remember that when you begin your deliberations. There is not a scintilla of other testimony or tangible proof that points to the defendant's guilt."

"Of necessity then, I trust that you will sincerely give your utmost attention to Karl Wainwright's testimony. I suggest that if you have reasonable doubt as to the truthfulness of his testimony, you must reasonably doubt the defendant's guilt, and, accordingly vote to acquit. There is simply no other evidence. And what is the quality of Karl Wainwright's evidence? What is his credibility as a witness?"

"Here is a man who arguably had more motive than the defendant to kill his father. Since the defendant was not legally married to the victim, Karl had every reason in the world to believe he was his father's sole heir and beneficiary. It says much, does it not, that Karl was excluded from every known version of the will? Do you not find this a bit odd? What might have passed between father and son to yield such an outcome?" Casey was leading the jurors to speculation, and several barely perceptible nods indicated at least a few were following. She had leeway in closing argument that would not have been permitted in the evidentiary portion of the trial. The judge would caution the jurors that statements made by the lawyers in closing did not constitute evidence.

Casey continued. "And what motive did Karl Wainwright have to render truthful testimony. For that we must rely upon our belief in his unfailing integrity. Otherwise what was Karl's sole chance to inherit his father's estate?" Casey let the jurors ponder the question a moment. "Yes, the defendant's guilt is Karl's only avenue to succeed to his father's estate." Casey gestured toward Celeste, who appeared properly demure and sinless. "Think about it. Are you willing to send this woman to the hangman based upon the testimony of Karl Wainwright?"

Casey briefly reviewed the holes and inconsistencies in Karl's testimony. How was the body removed from the house? Why was he not heard when he entered the house? Why did he wait so long before going to the sheriff? And, yes, where was the sheriff? Why did he not respond to the subpoena, leaving the defense without an important witness? She did not articulate it but strongly hinted at some dark reason for the sheriff's absence. Another suspect, perhaps? The blacksmith's eyes narrowed. He was wondering about that.

"Gentlemen of the jury, the judge will instruct you that the burden of proving the defendant's guilt rests upon the prosecution. She is not required to prove her innocence. That is not the way the American system of jurisprudence works. And I fear I may belabor the point, but the county attorney must prove the defendant's guilt beyond a reasonable doubt." She looked directly at the young schoolteacher. "A reasonable doubt." Then her eyes fixed on those of the husky blacksmith. "A reasonable doubt," she said in a near whisper as though the words were intended solely for his ears. And they were.

32

Casey

WHEN CASEY EMERGED from the town hall, it was with a sense of exhilaration. The case had been submitted to the jury, although since it was nearly mid-afternoon, the judge had declared deliberations would not commence until the next day. She had been a bit disappointed that Judge Hutchens denied her motion to sequester the jury, but she dared not argue the point too aggressively for fear of alienating jurors who wanted to return to their families and businesses before starting the process of deciding the case. Anyway, it was all out of her hands now, and she was not one to agonize over anything she could not change.

Her eyes narrowed against the glaring sunlight and she sneezed several times as she was prone to do whenever she came out of a building and encountered a blazing sun. She planned to return to her room at the Fremont and change into something more comfortable and then try to locate Ian. She expected her job in Borderview to be over before the weekend was out, and she needed to speak with him, although she had no idea what she was going to say. She admitted she had been avoiding Ian, not because she was embarrassed over the night they spent together, but more because she did not want to face the emotions he evoked in her. She was not a promiscuous woman. Other than her Comanche "husband" she had been intimate with only one other man before Ian, and her attraction to Ian Locke was a powerful thing, frighteningly so for a woman who was accustomed to being in control of her feelings.

As she approached The Fremont, Casey saw Emily engaged in conversation with a tall man on the boardwalk in front of the hotel. As she drew closer, she realized the man was Ian, attired in garb which seemed out of character for him. He was wearing a wide-brimmed, black hat, with a slender hatband adorned with gleaming silver concha at the base of the low crown. Several larger concha decorated a black leather vest slung over a bright red shirt that boasted a black string tie at the collar. The outfit was a bit flamboyant, she thought, but he did look dashing, and her heart raced at the prospect of their encounter.

Emily caught sight of her and waved. Ian looked her way and she could sense his appraisal with those steel-gray eyes that seemed uncharacteristically soft. Then she realized Ian was not Ian.

"Casey," Emily said, "I want you to meet Cam Locke, Ian's brother."

Cam tipped his hat with one hand and took hers in the other. "My distinct pleasure, ma'am. Emily's been telling me about your proficiency in the courtroom. I wish I'd got here for the show. I might have learned something."

Emily said, "I've got to run, Cam. I have to get today's story to the *Bee* by telegraph yet this afternoon." She turned to Casey. "First interview after the verdict? You'll give me time for a scoop?"

Casey smiled. "I may not be in a talking mood."

"Win or lose, Casey, you're the news. A woman lawyer handling a major murder case. This is a first in this state. Maybe in the entire country."

"I look to the day when being a woman has nothing to do with it."

Emily departed, leaving Casey and Cameron Locke standing on the boardwalk.

"I thought you were Ian when I first saw you," Casey remarked.

"How could you mistake us? He's older." Cam smiled warmly, and he had a perpetual twinkle in his eyes that she had seen only rarely in Ian's.

"You smile more."

"I don't take life quite so seriously as my brother. The Judge thinks I don't take things seriously enough. The Judge . . . that's what Ian and I call our father, behind his back."

"I know."

"You know?" Cam cocked his head and studied her with feigned seriousness. "I wonder if you're the trouble that brought me north?" He shook his head. "Nah, you're not big enough to cause that much trouble . . . on second thought—"

"What do you mean 'trouble?'"

"It can't really be explained. We don't talk about it much. Most folks would think we're crazy. But when one of us is troubled, dealing with something serious, the other seems to sense it. You just feel something's not right and need to check it out before you can rest easy."

"Is it always something terrible?"

"No, but when Ian was at Gettysburg . . . infantry, of

course . . . I had the feeling for a week. I was sick with worry, literally. I nearly puked up my guts for three days. I figured it out once and decided that was when he picked up the medal."

"Medal?"

"The big one. Medal of Honor. He didn't tell you? What am I saying? Of course not. He wouldn't have told even me if it hadn't been in the newspapers. And we've never kept much from each other."

"Emily told me he'd been in the war, but she never said anything about medals."

"I doubt if she knows. Wouldn't have learned it from him."

"So you're here because you had that feeling you talk about?"

"It didn't feel that serious, not like Gettysburg or when the boys took sick, but I thought I should head up this way. He wrote about us getting into the banking business, and I thought we ought to talk about that anyway. But I've been more concerned since I got off the train. I don't like what I'm feeling. As soon as I dropped my bedroll at the hotel I was going to hightail it over to Ian's office and satisfy myself he doesn't need a hand with something."

Casey shuddered. "You're making me spooky, Cam. I hope you're joshing me with this talk."

"I've been known to tease now and then, ma'am, but not right now."

"Cam," a voice yelled from down the street.

Casey turned to see Will Heasty racing up the street. He arrived out of breath. "Train came in early . . . missed you at the station . . . figured I might catch you here."

Cam Locke's face turned grim now. "Where's Ian?"

"That's why I was looking for you. I got word from George

Washington's son late this morning. Mandy was taken last night."

"Taken?'

"A man . . . they think it was Karl Wainwright . . . took her from the barn last night. Ian and George rode out in the storm to find her."

"Oh, my God," Casey gasped.

"Who's Karl Wainwright?"

Will replied. "A snake. I hate to say this, but he was suspected of raping and killing a young girl some five years back. Ian's come across information recently that lends support to the theory."

"Christ."

Casey asked, "Did you report it to the deputy?"

"No. Ian sent instructions. He asked that Cam go to the ranch and wait for word there. If he hasn't heard from Ian or George by nightfall, he's on his own."

"I'm heading for the livery," Cam said. "I'll rent a horse and head for the Lazy Key."

"Rent two horses," Casey said. "And swing back here. I'm going with you. I'll change and be ready to ride by the time you get here."

Cam started to protest, saw the fire in her eyes, and decided against it.

33

Ian

GEORGE WENT OUTSIDE to look around, sensing I needed some quiet time, a chance to pull myself together. Grief and rage boiled within me, and I knew I had to get a handle on it. That kind of stew was no good for the job that lay ahead. I looked around the stark, dirty shack and tried not to imagine the horror Mandy must have endured here. I found her boots and socks in a corner and gathered up her clothes. I would put them in the saddlebags. One way or another we would need them.

Momentarily, George returned. "Come outside," he said. "You need to take a look at this."

I followed obediently. Outside the cabin door he pointed to tracks that were now interspersed with our own. There was a pair of bare footprints in the drying mud. "Mandy's," I commented.

"Looks like it. And you've got her boots in your hands. She must have come out here after the boots came off. Come back here." He motioned me to the back of the shack. "Did you see the paw prints?"

"I see them now."

"Cat."

"Bobcat?"

"Tillie Crump kind of cat."

I thought of something. "You know, I never saw TJ when I went out to the barn. He was with Mandy. You don't suppose—"

"Possible."

"I can't imagine. We're a long way from home."

George shrugged. "Their horses were tied back here. Two of them. One rider rode out ahead of the other. I'd guess Mandy was on that one." He walked toward the west side of the shack, and then he stooped and plucked an object from the grass. "Blood in the grass near where this horse was staked. And I just found this." He held out a rusty, blood-caked awl.

I shook my head in puzzlement. "What do you make of it?"

"I think that's Karl Wainwright's blood we saw, not Mandy's. I think she found this awl, and I don't think she was punching belt holes or fixing a saddle with it."

"Let's ride."

George and I decided to ride the spare mounts and give our other horses a rest, and I rode Dancer now, as Hemlock trailed behind. We picked our way down the canyon, dodging mud holes and avoiding slippery banks. The rain had softened the canyon floor, and George's tracking skills were not required to follow the trail left by the other horses. The canyon clotted with young cottonwoods and sand willows and other undergrowth as we moved southward, however, and the going got tougher.

No more than a mile down the canyon, we turned a corner in the canyon wall and came upon a horse flattened on its side and flailing helplessly in the rock and sand. We dismounted and hurried to the mare's side. She tried to raise her head and stared at us with pain-filled eyes. "Foreleg's broken," I said. "Can't shoot her. Karl would hear and know we're on his trail . . . if he doesn't already."

George slipped his Bowie knife from its sheath and quickly ended the animal's misery. Then he began to circle the ground and brush around the dead horse, nose nearly to the ground like a damned bloodhound. I did my part by staying out of his way. I lost sight of him for a spell, and then suddenly he materialized silently from the undergrowth not more than a dozen feet from where I stood. The old savage was reverting to his youth, I thought.

"Mandy's horse," he said softly. "I found her footprints. Damned if those cat tracks didn't show up, too, further up the trail. Karl's on foot now, too, leading his horse. We'd better tie our horses here and follow afoot. They can't gain ground on us if they're not moving on horseback. Karl will pick us off like a couple of fat prairie hens if we go crashing through the trees."

Suddenly, a mournful yowling echoed off the canyon walls. It faded, and a few moments later it erupted again, followed by a gunshot that reverberated like a cannon off the rocky palisades. Undaunted, the creature yowled again.

"That's TJ," I said.

We yanked our rifles from the saddle holsters and began working our way downstream. The canyon floor changed to near solid sandstone as we inched southward, and it became more difficult to find sign. When we did, the tracks appeared to be crisscrossing and weaving in no predictable pattern, so we agreed to split again and work separate sides of the stream. Our progress was discouraging until I heard TJ yowl again and knew we had closed the gap significantly.

34

Mandy

AMANDA KATE LOCKE huddled in a fetal position in a concave cavity that had been carved by time at the base of the sandstone canyon wall. Her hiding place extended no more than five feet into the stone, but was protected by a shield of tall switch grass and brush and willows. She had stretched her filthy shirt down her thighs and over her knees, not because it was cold in her hideaway, but because it somehow made her feel safer. The right side of her face was scarlet fading to purple and her eye was swollen shut. Her lower lip protruded like a spoiled grape and leaked blood.

She reached down and stroked the mud-caked cat that was curled up next to her. TJ seemed unruffled by their ordeal and slept blissfully and seemingly unconcerned about the horrid man who stalked them. At least while he slept he was quiet. She had feared the racket TJ was making earlier, as he sought her out, would lead the "albino" to her hiding place, but the man had evidently taken a shot at the cat and scared him into hiding. Mentally, she had anointed Karl Wainwright the "albino" because she did not know his given name and his ghostly-pale skin and bleached-out blond hair made her think of a story she had once read about an albino man. Even his pale-blue eyes were nearly colorless.

TJ had saved her, though, and given her the opportunity she had prayed for. The albino had not even bothered to unsaddle the horses before he drug her into the cabin and threw her on the floor. When she tried to rush for the open doorway, he had struck her again and tossed her on the rickety cot and then gone back outside, presumably to relieve himself. That was when she spotted the awl on the windowsill and retrieved it and slipped it under the straw mattress. When he returned, he was smiling, licking his lips. She had seen that expression before on Victor's face when he came to her room in the darkness of the night, while he thought she slept, and touched her breasts and private places with one hand and caressed his bloated spear with the other.

She had remained sitting on the cot as the albino crept toward her, loosening his belt as he approached. When he reached for her, she made a final lunge to get past him, but he latched onto her arm like a vise and yanked her back, and his fist came down like a hammer on her mouth. Dazed, she fell back on the cot and only vaguely remembered now that her boots and britches and underpants were being stripped away. As she regained her senses she saw the albino struggling with his own trousers, dropping them to his ankles and then suddenly freeing his erect, swaying monster.

It was then that TJ yowled from outside the door and began rattling it with his paws. Startled, the albino cursed and turned his head toward the door. In that instant she slipped her hand under the mattress. Her fingers closed on the awl's handle and she pulled it out. The moment the albino turned his attention back to her, she struck at his groin with an underhanded stab that tore into his spear. He shrieked in agony and his eyes widened in horror, and before he could grasp what happened she rose up and drove the awl's point into his lower abdoman. In his panic to escape the surprise attack, the albino backed away, screaming hysterically, got his feet tangled in his fallen trousers and tumbled over backwards onto the floor with the awl still lodged in his belly, blood oozing around its rusty tine. That was her final image of the albino as she darted out the door and raced for the horses.

Mandy's thoughts turned now to the horse. It pained her to think of leaving the injured mare alone in her distress. She knew there was nothing she could have done for the animal, but it was sad that there was no one to comfort the creature, sadder still that no one could bring an end to the mare's misery. Mandy faulted herself for pushing the horse too hard. If she had been more patient, she might have seen the treacherous sinkhole that had been filled and camouflaged by the recent rains. She had only been bruised and shaken when the mare thrust forward in her fall. She had scooped up TJ when she escaped the shack and stuffed him in the saddlebags where he usually traveled, but he had been nearly squashed when the horse went down and had taken off like a thunderbolt after he squirmed free.

Mandy crawled to the opening of the shallow cave and looked out. The sun glowed at high noon. Her father would be searching for her. George and, perhaps others, too. But with all the rain, there would be no trail. She couldn't count on help. She didn't know how badly she had hurt the albino, but apparently not badly enough, because she had heard him calling for her, promising her he would take her home, assuring her no harm would come to her. And he had fired a shot at TJ.

She had two choices: run or wait it out. Her father had told her if she ever got lost to stay put for as long as she could. She was less likely to be found if she was on the move. On the other hand, if after taking time to collect her wits, common sense told her she should leave her spot, she should always stay with the water. Come to a stream; follow it. Sooner or later, the stream will empty into a creek, and the creek will make its way to a river. Even if it takes days, the water will flow to people. That's where folks live: where there's water.

She had the stream to follow not more than fifty yards away, but it was too risky to expose herself in daylight. If the albino couldn't find her today, maybe he would give up. If he did locate her, she knew he would do terrible things to her, things she had heard about when she and her friends back in Omaha had laughed and giggled about the wicked things men did with their spears, although she had never found it truly funny, because she knew about sick things that she would never have told her friends. Mandy also knew the albino would kill her when he was finished with her. She would wait till nightfall, she decided. Then she would leave her hiding place and follow the stream.

She started to move further back into the cave when she heard something moving noisily through the undergrowth, something that was making no effort to move quietly. It was the albino. She knew it was. The sound was moving closer and closer. He must have found her footprints. She decided to run.

Too late. The albino stepped from behind the trees, his rifle aimed directly at her. "Don't run, little rabbit," Karl Wainwright said in a near whisper. "You're in my sights. My old man didn't teach me much, but he taught me to shoot with the best. I'm finished chasing you."

As the albino moved closer, Mandy saw that the front and legs of his trousers were blood-soaked, and he was staggering more than walking, wincing in pain with each step he took. If it were not for his rifle, she could run and he wouldn't catch her in a hundred years.

Out of the corner of her eye, Mandy saw TJ streak out of the cave. The albino caught sight of him, too, and took a bead on the cat with his gun before the animal disappeared into the tall grass.

"Well, little rabbit, I guess we've had a change of plans," Karl said, as he limped toward her. "You and me got a score to settle before I head for civilization. You hurt me bad . . . real bad. You're going to hurt, too, before I'm done with you."

When he reached the mouth of the cave, Mandy backed away, watching for her opportunity. She could hear TJ yowling like a bobcat in the brush a short distance away. She knew the albino intended to kill her and that he did not have an easy death in mind. She had to make a break for it—and soon. When he was within five feet of her, Karl stopped and stared at her for some moments with glazed eyes, and then he shifted his rifle to his right hand and lunged for Mandy, grabbing her arm and yanking her toward him. She feigned surrender before suddenly pulling away and breaking free of his grasp.

"Bitch," he yelled, as he whipped the rifle barrel around and struck a glancing blow on her head, catapulting her from the cave entrance and onto the rocky ground outside.

Karl walked slowly to where Mandy lay, dazed and bleeding and struggling to get back on her feet, but unable to summon the strength. He leaned his rifle against a tree and stuck a hand in his trousers and fished out a small penknife. "This will serve the purpose," he said, as he pressed out the blade

"Stop right there," came a firm menacing voice. Mandy recognized it instantly as her father's.

Karl Wainwright turned to face Ian Locke moving deliberately toward him along the base of the canyon wall. Karl dropped the knife and started to reach for his rifle and then thought better of it when he saw the Colt revolver leveled steadily at his midsection and the smoldering eyes of its bearer. He stepped away from the gun and raised his hands. "I'm not armed. I'm not armed," he whined. "You can't shoot an unarmed man."

"Is that right?" Locke said, as he lowered the pistol, squeezed the trigger and fired a bullet into Karl Wainwright's right kneecap.

35

Ian

KARL WAINWRIGHT WRITHED in pain, sobbing and moaning, as he tried to staunch the blood that streamed through the fingers that clutched his shattered knee. I picked up the man's rifle and slung it safely out of reach. "Stay put," I said needlessly, as I knelt at my daughter's side.

I placed my hand gently under Mandy's head and raised it slightly, and her eyes fluttered open. "Dad," she mumbled. "I knew you'd come."

I tugged a kerchief from my pocket and wiped the blood away from her scalp. A nasty gash. Doc Mason might need to take some stitches to close the wound—or George could do it in a pinch. I took off my shirt and ripped it into strips with my knife and then fashioned crude compresses to seal the laceration. Momentarily, George appeared with TJ following not far behind.

George's dark eyes took in the scene. "I heard the gunshot. Looks like it was yours."

"I disabled the bastard. He won't give us any more trouble. I got here just in time. He was going to take a knife to her. If I hadn't heard TJ yowling out there in the timber, I might have been too late."

Mandy slowly lifted herself to a sitting position. She was filthy and bruised and blood-spattered, and I thought her the most beautiful creature I had ever seen. I clutched her to my chest and held her, and she shuddered and suddenly let loose with a mournful wail that turned to wave after wave of unrelenting sobbing. My own tears streamed silently down my cheeks as I stroked her hair softly and repeated again and again, "It's all right, Princess. It's over. It's all right."

George gathered up the remains of Locke's shirt and left for a short time. When he returned, he had the horses in tow. He handed a canteen and some wet rags to me and then walked over to Karl Wainwright, who leaned against a sandstone boulder weeping and groaning in agony, his previously pale face now drained of all remnants of color.

"Help me. Help me," Karl pleaded.

George spat a gooey string of tobacco in the man's face. "Shall I finish him off, Ian?"

"No, he and I need to have a chat. See if you can stem the blood flow. I'd just as soon he didn't bleed to death ... yet."

Mandy's composure slowly returned, and I encouraged her to slowly sip at the canteen while I washed the dirt and blood from her face and arms. I retrieved her clothes from the saddlebags and suggested she put on her things. When she was dressed, I thought, with the exception of her battered face and head, she seemed physically the same old Mandy. I could not bring himself to ask the question that weighed most heavily on my mind.

TJ came over and rubbed against Mandy's legs, purring as if this were just another routine day in cat life. "TJ is a hero, Dad. He saved my life. He made a racket outside the shack just when . . . and it startled the albino and gave me a chance to get the sharp tool and stab him."

"The albino?"

"That's what I called him in my head. I didn't know who he was. Do you know him?"

I looked over at the weakened form of Karl Wainwright. George had used an ash stick and a strip of cloth from my shirt to improvise a tourniquet above the knee. The blood flow had ebbed noticeably. "Yes, Mandy, I know him."

George came over and placed a gentle hand on Mandy's swollen face. "We're sure glad to finally catch up with you. I think you made that hombre wish he'd never tangled with a Locke, though." He turned to me with a glint of humor in his eyes. "What you did to Karl's knee is nothing compared to what this young lady did to his privates. I think smart folks would think twice and maybe a third time before taking on one of your kin."

I was in no mood to banter. "I want Mandy home before nightfall. And with swollen creeks and mud, it might take some time to get there. I'd like you to take Mandy to the Lazy Key and leave her off if Cam's there. Maybe you could send Willow or Martha over to see to her till I get home. I won't be far behind. If Cam's not there, take her to your place."

"I have a better idea. Why don't you take her back? She's been through a lot. She needs to be with her father now. I'll stay behind and have that little talk with Mr. Wainwright."

My eyes met George's evenly. "We've already settled this, George. Debate's closed."

36

Casey

CASEY McGLAUN AND Cameron Locke sat on leather-upholstered chairs in the parlor of the Lazy Key ranch house. They sipped at cups of coffee, poured from a steaming pot Cam had brewed after their arrival. Both fidgeted nervously and took turns getting up and peering out the window, as if that would somehow speed up the arrival of Ian and Mandy. While Ian Locke was a man of patience and persistence, Mandy noted Cam Locke was obviously more impulsive and inclined to action, damn the consequences.

Physically, the twins were mirror images, but, temperamentally, there were great differences. Cam was a gregarious man who moved comfortably among strangers, smiled easily and, under normal circumstances, would be fairly easily seduced from work to play, Casey surmised. He rode like a Comanche born to a horse, and their race to the ranch had given way to an undeclared competition, which Casey narrowly won, she remembered with a measure of satisfaction.

As they waited in the parlor, Casey told Cam what she knew about Karl Wainwright and the role he had played in the trial and explained how she had come to know Ian Locke—but not how well she knew him. "Ian's a very interesting man," she remarked.

Cam cocked his head and studied her appraisingly. This tilting of his head when he pondered something was a charming mannerism, Casey thought, but it also put her on guard, because it frequently preceded some outlandish observation.

"Are you in love with my brother, Casey?"

She was not easily surprised, but the question took her unaware. She hesitated some moments before responding. "A rather personal question, don't you think?"

He gave her a sheepish, boyish smile that smothered any annoyance she might have harbored. "Yeah, I suppose so. Are you?"

"I don't know. I haven't had time to really examine my feelings about your brother."

"Well, it won't do any good to analyze it like a lawyer tearing into a legal problem. Ian's the family philosopher, but I know a few things about love, and I can tell you it's not susceptible to rational examination. So forget about that. When the idea of living your life without that other person drives you insane, you'll know you're dealing with love and fighting a losing battle. Best give in to it at that point."

"It's nice to be able to get advice from an expert."

"I've been smitten by the same woman for fifteen years now. I cannot imagine life without her. She's a gifted artist among other things. That's one of her paintings above the mantle."

Casey studied the painting. She had admired it on her previous visit and had meant to inquire about it. The setting was Weeping Springs and Mushroom Rock. An Indian warrior, clad only in breechcloth sat on a stone shelf, back propped against a tree. His sinewy-muscled buttocks and thighs peered from beneath his loincloth, and angry red scars from battles past marred an otherwise perfect body. His weary eyes were locked with those of a maiden scantily clad in buckskins who was picking up his bow and quiver, her dark eyes warm, seductive. The artist favored rich pigments and sharply drawn subjects. The painting evoked a strange mix of emotions, melancholy and sadness, hope and love, all woven with a thread of eroticism cast against a backdrop of wild, stunning beauty.

"She called it 'Warrior's Return.' She and the kids came with me on a visit a few years back. When Pilar got a glimpse of Weeping Springs, she had to take her easel and paints down to the springs. She did several paintings with that setting, but this one was especially for Ian."

"She has a rare talent."

"She's a rare woman."

"Tell me about Ian and the war. I sense that it was somehow defining for him."

"I think war is defining for most men who experience it. Everything in your lifetime either happened before the war or after the war. It's a benchmark. But some men, maybe because of their unique encounters or just because of the men they are, carry more ghosts than others."

"And Ian carries ghosts."

"Oh, yes. As you know, Ian was at Gettysburg. He fought with the Eighth Ohio infantry near Cemetery Ridge. He'd made sergeant by this time, and by afternoon of that day, he was the only officer of any kind left in his company. He received orders to hold a slope that led to the crest of the ridge at all costs. If you know Ian, you know he's damn stubborn when he makes up his mind. He had his men dig in on that hill . . . no more than thirty of them. When the Confederates began their advance, there were close to three hundred gray suits moving up that hill. Time after time, Ian's men beat back the charge. It went on for hours and Ian's soldiers dropped one by one till there were just a few left. The Confederates regrouped for a final bayonet charge and they finally overran the Eighth's position. The newspapers said Ian personally killed over fifteen Confederates by saber, bayonet and pistol in that final charge, that bodies were piled around him like sandbags. Then Federal artillery fire targeted the hillside and the enemy ranks broke and crumbled and they ran for safety. Ian and three other men from his company survived. The other survivors were badly wounded. Ian didn't have a scratch on him. I don't think he ever forgave himself for that."

"My God. I suppose he does wonder why he lived to remember it."

"Yep. He fought the whole damn war that way. Like he was untouchable. Maybe he used up all his luck during those years. Since then he's lost the boys and a marriage, faced financial ruin . . . and now this. Me, I took a few Yankee mini-balls during the war . . . still got one lodged in my back . . . but otherwise the saints have blessed me. Two fine sons and a daughter who have never had more than the sniffles. A wife who can melt me with a wink."

"You fought for the South?"

"Yes, ma'am. Cavalry. I rode with General James Ewell Brown Stuart. Old Jeb. I was at Gettysburg too. But that's another story."

"The two of you are different."

"We don't think so much different. Ian and I almost always come to the same conclusions. We just get there different ways sometimes. The war was an exception, but even that had more to do with where we lived at the time than what we believed in. Ian and I never had nastiness over our personal choices, but I'm not sure the Judge has forgiven me yet for being a Johnny Reb."

"You're not nearly as intense as Ian."

"He was always the serious one. It's funny. Not more than a few minutes separated our births, but the Judge and Mother both anointed Ian firstborn and burdened him with all the responsibilities that go with it. I always got by with more when we were growing up. Ian was the scholar, the writer. Oh, I never had a problem with school, but I never had as much expected of me. I always had more fun. Still do."

"It's amazing you've stayed so close."

"It's always been that way. Strangely, we never fought like most brothers. We just pursued our own interests, went our own ways. But Ian . . . next to Pilar . . . is my best friend. And I know I'm his best friend, although I wouldn't begrudge him another." He looked at Casey meaningfully.

Casey got up and poured another cup of coffee and stepped over to the window, surveying the undulating waves of grass that danced over the rolling hills to the south. "What if something terrible happens to Mandy? What will that do to him?"

Cam spoke in a voice that was just above a whisper. "The man who does her harm will never know a night's rest. The word 'quit' is not in Ian's vocabulary. Ian would hunt him down like an animal."

"Would he kill him?"

"Yes. I think so."

"But he's a lawyer. He's an officer of the court."

Cam shrugged.

"After that," Casey said. "After he did whatever he decided to do with the man. What then?"

"Some way he would persevere. He would go on. People endure terrible things, but somehow most eventually pull themselves together and go on down the road of life. Not a happy road, perhaps, but they survive."

"He's due for a change of luck, wouldn't you think?"

"If ever a man deserved it, my brother does."

Casey caught sight of movement in the distance, barely discernible objects skirting the steeper hills and winding their ways like tiny ants in the direction of the farmstead. "Cam," she said. "There are riders headed this way."

The two of them rushed out onto the veranda and watched together as the riders came into view. Two riders and a spare horse. Casey could feel her heart racing. There should be three. When the riders galloped into the yard, Casey and Cam ran out to greet them. George and, thank God, Mandy, with TJ clinging to the saddle in front of her. But where was Ian? Her heart sank with cold fear.

At the sight of Cam, Mandy stared at him quizzically, and then gave a half-smile with the side of her mouth that was not swollen. "You're Uncle Cam, aren't you?"

"That I am, young lady," Cam replied as he reached up and plucked her off Dancer, with TJ clutched in her arms, and carried her toward the house.

"You're not more handsome than my dad."

Cam laughed loudly. "I think your old man's been poisoning your mind, young lady. You just haven't seen me gussied up yet."

Casey held back and spoke with George. "Ian?"

"He'll be along."

"It was Karl?"

George nodded.

"And you caught him? Where is he?"

"He's having a visit with Ian."

"A visit?"

"Yes, ma'am."

"Will Ian be taking him to the sheriff?"

"Can't say. But I think it's more likely Karl will be taking a trip down the river . . . with the flooding, New Orleans, maybe."

"I don't understand." But then she did.

"Ma'am, I'm going to mosey over to my place and have the women folk fix me up a hot tub. Then I'm going to eat till I'm near sick. I'll send Willow and Rosemary over with some grub. But I'm done answering questions for the day. I'd just like to leave you with a bit of advice."

"What's that?"

"When Ian comes back, forget you're a lawyer. No questions. Ever. But hold him close. He could use that."

37

Ian

I UNSADDLED HEMLOCK and tethered him in a lush meadow that edged the stream. The big gelding had served me well and had been on his best behavior, so he was entitled to a respite before we headed back to the Lazy Key. Besides, I was in no particular hurry to deal with the unpleasant business that faced me.

I found Karl Wainwright's bay mare hitched in some plum thickets about a hundred yards from Mandy's hideout, and I removed saddle and bridle from the animal and set her free. She carried the brand of a livery that operated out of Apple Center, a village some five miles west of here, and she would likely show up at a neighboring farmer or rancher's place and eventually get delivered to her rightful owner. I would have George make discreet inquiries and anonymously make it right with the livery if the animal didn't return to inventory.

I had left Karl whimpering on the rocky ground in front of the cave opening, and having tended to the horses, I made my way back now to address remaining issues with Mandy's abductor. As I approached the suffering man, I noted that Karl had not budged an inch in the half hour or so that had passed during my absence, not that there was much chance he would get far with the mangled knee. I kicked off some rotting edges on an old tree stump and made myself a seat a dozen feet from the injured man. Karl watched me with terror-filled eyes as I positioned myself on the stump.

I slipped my colt from its holster and punched a cartridge in the vacant chamber. I sighted the pistol at Karl's head and then lowered it, letting the weapon dangle loosely in my hand. "I'm going to ask some questions," I told him. "You're going to answer."

"I'm hurt. I'm hurt bad. I need a sawbones. I'm not saying anything unless you promise to take me to a doctor." The man tried to straighten his back in a desperate act of defiance, but yelped in pain when he tried to shift his body against his stone backrest.

"I don't think you understand, Karl. You have no cards. Not one." I pointed the pistol at the man again. "Now you can buy yourself some time. Take a chance that my kinder nature will win out. Or we can just get it over with and I can be on my way."

Karl Wainwright's eyes seemed to search mine for a clue, and I suspect he found no mercy there. His brief flirtation with bravado collapsed. "You're insane. You'd kill an unarmed man? In cold blood?"

"No more than you'd rape and murder an innocent girl."

"What do you want to know?"

"You raped and murdered the Morgan girl five years ago, didn't you?"

Silence.

"It doesn't matter. I see the truth in your eyes. And, of course,

Ike Bell figured it out and helped you suck your father dry with blackmail. How many more girls, Karl? St. Louis would be paradise for a man like you. Orphans. Passers through. Hundreds of young girls who might never be missed. Not enough law to track the killer if they are." I paused before I spoke. "I tell you what, Karl. I really just want to satisfy my curiosity about a few things I'm not sure of. And I don't have time to waste. I'd like to head home and be with my little girl. You know her, don't you? Mandy? The one you've been stalking for days? The one you took away and beat and defiled? But I'm digressing. What I'd like to know concerns your father's murder. Now here's the game we're going to play. I'll ask a question. If you refuse to answer . . . or lie . . . I'll put a bullet in your other knee. Then I'll ask again. If I get the same response, the bullet goes in your brain and I go home. Understood?"

Karl shook his head and moaned in agony and began to sob uncontrollably again.

"Did you kill your father, Karl?"

"No," Karl whimpered.

"I believe you." I lowered my pistol again. "It was Celeste, wasn't it?"

"Yes. It was mostly like I said at the trial . . . except I was there from the beginning. My father was dead drunk. We had been sitting in the kitchen arguing before he passed out. Celeste tried to get me to kill him but I couldn't . . . he was my father after all."

"So Celeste shot him?"

"Yes."

"And you helped her dispose of the body?"

"Me and the sheriff."

"Ike?"

"Yes. Celeste didn't know. But after we got father in the buckboard, she washed her hands of it. Told me to get rid of the body . . . but to be sure somebody found it. I didn't know what to do, so I went to Ike. I promised I'd keep him on the payroll if I ended up with the estate. Mrs. Crump's pigpen was his idea. Celeste threw a fit when I told her I'd dropped the body in the pigpen. Said if the hogs ate father, there wouldn't be a corpse to prove he was dead and that would complicate things. Fortunately, you and Mrs.Crump came along. I never told her about Ike helping me . . . and Ike made me promise I wouldn't tell."

"Whose idea was it for you to come forth to testify against Celeste?"

"It was Ike's. When he heard about the handwritten will, he came to me and suggested I turn Celeste in. I'd be pointing to the real killer and she couldn't pull me into it without confessing her part. Once she was convicted nobody would believe her, and Ike said he'd alibi for me anyway. It looked like I might get the estate if they hung Celeste or sent her to prison."

I stared at the pistol in my hand for some moments and then got up and walked over and looked down at Karl's pathetic form. I bent over and unfastened the man's belt buckle and yanked Karl's trousers down to his thighs, as he squealed in misery. I flinched at the grotesque wounds I uncovered. Already the man's groin was inflamed and distended, the tender flesh turning raw and rancid, and his mangled penis drooped limp and bulbous between his blood-smeared thighs, probably unable to pass urine, I thought. Blood still oozed from the shattered knee, but it would take another day for gangrene to set in. Karl looked up at me with feverish, pleading eyes. His semi-confession had seemingly sapped the last of his reserves, and his torment had driven him to surrender. I pressed the cold barrel of the Colt to Karl Wainwright's temple.

38

Ian

WHEN I STEPPED out of the saddle and led Hemlock to the hitching post in front of the house, I was startled to find Casey standing in the shadows of the veranda. She moved swiftly down the porch steps and was in my arms before I realized what was happening. I held her tightly and desperately, drinking of her touch and warmth and scent, vaguely aware my own scent might not carry similar comfort. Our lips met, first lightly, then hungrily.

"Mandy's sleeping," she said in an unnecessary whisper. "Cam's in repose on the floor of the parlor. Let me help you put Hemlock up." She took the gelding's reins, and both horse and man trailed her to the stable.

Casey tended to Hemlock with quiet efficiency, and neither of us spoke while I watched her grain and rub down the grateful animal, docile as a sleepy kitten under her expert care. The horse settled in, Casey took my hand and led me to an empty stall where I discovered someone had fashioned an inviting bed of fresh straw and blankets. I learned I was not quite as exhausted as I thought and let the ever-persuasive redhead have her way with me.

I don't know when I dropped off to sleep, but it was sudden and dead, and I was disoriented when Casey shook me awake in the middle of the night. Feeling her taut nipples brushing my naked back, I rolled over to oblige. "Not that," she said, gently pushing me away. "Well, not this minute, anyway. We need to talk. About Mandy."

I sat up and she snuggled in beside me, resting her head on my shoulder and pulling a blanket around us. "She is all right, isn't she? You would have told me—"

"She's doing unbelievably well under the circumstances."

I waited for her to continue and cast my eyes about the stable, dusky in the soft moonlight that crept through the windows. With this woman at my side, it was a poor man's heaven. Casey remained silent, so I asked, "Should she see a doctor?"

"It probably wouldn't hurt, but I stitched her scalp wound, and Cam and I applied some of your vet salves to her swollen eye and lips. I helped her with a hot bath, and Willow brought over some soup and fresh bread . . . which you would probably enjoy yourself."

"The soup or the bath?"

She snuffed her nose a bit crudely I thought. "You could certainly stand a bath"

"Will you help me with it?" That remark earned a soft punch in the ribs. "Seriously," I said, "I'm grateful you were here for Mandy. You stitched her scalp? You didn't tell me you were a physician, too."

"Comanche women learn very early about sewing up wounds. I've dealt with much worse."

"There is something I need to know."

"You want to know if Karl violated her?"

"Don't want to know. *Need* to know."

"He did not."

"You're certain?"

"Yes, he was going to rape her when she attacked him. Ian, Mandy is an incredibly brave young lady. Resourceful and tough. And I think she is one of those special persons who will grow from adversity rather than be destroyed by it."

"Like you."

"Perhaps. But I was thinking of her father. We had a long talk. Or I should say, Mandy talked. I mostly listened. I assured her she could speak to me in confidence, and I will respect that. But I asked her permission to discuss one issue with you, and she consented."

"This sounds ominous."

"Ominous portends future. This is past. And we have to keep it there. It's about her stepfather . . . and by acquiescence, her mother."

"Victor?"

"He's been molesting her."

"The bastard." I started to get up, but Casey held me back. "The son of a bitch. I can't believe this."

"There is no way to minimize what he's done, but so far, his behavior hasn't gone beyond nighttime fondling or touching while he thinks Mandy is sleeping. But she has seen him stroking what she calls his 'spear' during these episodes. She relates his conduct to her experience with Karl, and now she's terrified at the thought of living in the same house as Victor."

"She needn't be," I said. The thought of that vile son of a

bitch touching my daughter in that way triggered waves of nausea in my stomach and forced bile into my throat. This just wasn't possible. "She won't be living anywhere with Victor Hampton again. She won't be within a hundred yards of him."

"I can help you with that if you want. The Omaha courts have jurisdiction of the case. I can file an application for change of custody on your behalf. Perhaps, when Nadine returns, you can confront her and propose an arrangement that wouldn't put Mandy in the middle of a custody battle."

"Did Nadine know about this? Did Mandy tell her mother?"

"She said she tried, but she didn't know how to explain it. She told her mother that he came to her room and touched her at night, but she was afraid to be explicit . . . didn't really know how to express it. Nadine just shrugged it off . . . said Victor was just showing his affection."

"She's nuts."

"Blind, I suppose. People have great ability to deny things they don't want to believe. But Nadine became a believer one night when she followed Victor to Mandy's room and caught him in the act, so to speak. Mandy said there was a terrible fight and that Nadine threatened to summon the law. They returned to their own bedroom and carried on their battle through the night. The next morning, Nadine behaved as though nothing had happened and never spoke of the incident. A month later, her mother announced she and Victor were going to Europe and that Mandy would not be accompanying them. Mandy, of course, by this time was not interested in traveling anywhere with Victor, but she begged her mother not to go. Nadine just declared she and Victor needed time together. I gather this was an effort to save the marriage, but I can't imagine why."

"Because you haven't been raised in Nadine's society. First, Victor's money and status are hugely important to Nadine. Her family never quite forgave her for marrying down when she exchanged vows with a young, penniless lawyer. Divorce is a horrible disgrace among her set. Your husband can beat you; he can have a dozen mistresses; but you stay married. She has about lived down one divorce. But two? In her own mind a second divorce would be nearly unthinkable."

"But her daughter's well- being—"

"She does love Mandy. That's why she didn't take her to Europe. It had to be a gut-wrenching decision for Nadine to leave Mandy in my care."

"But she knew she was safe with you. Deep down she knows the kind of man you are."

"I don't even know what kind of man I am. But I'd never let harm come to my daughter. Never."

"Mandy wants to stay with you. She wants to live here."

"She told you that?"

"Yes, in spite of what's happened, she's never been so happy. She worships you. She knows you'll take care of her. She wants to see her mother when Victor's not with her. But she wants to stay here, even if Nadine divorces Victor."

I couldn't deny my indescribable joy at the thought of Mandy remaining with me at the Lazy Key, and still I felt an undeniable sadness for Nadine's sake. "It won't be easy, but we'll make it happen."

I kissed the top of Casey's head and with my fingertips tilted her face toward mine, looking into her eyes. "You look very thoughtful," she said teasingly.

"I'm debating about whether to risk making an ass of

myself."

Her eyes narrowed suspiciously. "You haven't seemed all that adverse to risk-taking in the short time I've known you."

I blurted it out. "I'd like you to stay here, too."

Her eyes widened in disbelief. The unflappable Casey McGlaun had shock written all over her face.

"Stay here?"

"I'm asking you to marry me. I love you, Casey."

"I . . . I don't know what to say."

"How about 'yes?'"

"It's not that simple."

"You don't feel the same way?"

"Ian, I've never felt about any man the way I've come to feel about you. I think we can have an unbelievable friendship. As a lover . . . well, if there's ever another he's doomed to be a disappointment to me in comparison to what we've shared."

"But you aren't in love with me?"

"I'm not trying to be evasive. I'm not sure what love is. What I feel for you is very, very powerful . . . it's almost frightening to me."

"Why?"

"Because I have dreams, Ian. And if I married you, I'd have to give them up."

"I don't see why. Dreams change anyway. They're not reality. That's why we call them dreams. I've been replacing old dreams with new ones all of my life."

"I want to be the best trial lawyer west of the Missouri."

"You can do that. I know Will would be agreeable to you joining our firm. He'd welcome the companionship since I decided yesterday I'm going to take a leave of absence and be a banker for a while . . . at least until I sort out a few other things in my mind. With rails reaching almost every place these days, Borderview could be home and you could travel to where your cases take you. After all the newspaper coverage about Celeste's trial, win or lose, clients will find you . . . no more beating the bushes for your next case."

"That remains to be seen." Her eyes met mine for a long moment, and I saw genuine sorrow there. She sat up and started to fumble in the straw for her undergarments. "I'm sorry, Ian. I truly am. I've never intended to marry. Being a lawyer is my life. There's not room for anything else long-term."

39

Casey

THE JURY HAD deliberated only about five hours when the judge was notified a verdict had been reached. Court was convened again in the town hall, and the judge, lawyers and spectators waited now for the jurors to be escorted by the bailiff from Reuben's county courtroom where they had been sequestered for deliberations. Celeste sat silently next to Casey at the defense table, her bearing cool and supremely confident. Their greetings had been brief and perfunctory. Casey did not much like her client and was sure Celeste held no particular affection for her. Their relationship was business and professional, and unless the jury's decision mandated an appeal, Casey expected to employ Will Heasty to handle collection of her fees and hoped never to see Celeste Kimball, or whatever her name was, after this day.

Casey would not have been in a mood to chat with any client this Friday afternoon, or any person for that matter. Last night's ending with Ian had left her in a rare funk. If only he had not asked her to marry him so soon, pushed her to a decision, perhaps they would have had some time to see where their relationship would lead. Of course, she was returning to Omaha tomorrow, and she supposed that would have been the end of it in any event.

At least they had parted without unpleasantness. Ian had accepted her verdict, much as she must accept the jury's in a few moments. He had been silent and stoic as they dressed, but she sensed no anger or resentment in his manner, certainly no plea for sympathy. He had helped her saddle her horse, rendering only a token protest when she insisted upon riding out into the pitch black of night to make her return journey to town alone, and he had kissed her before she left, although a bit too chastely. Yes, he did understand her—and totally embraced her as she was. She did not expect to meet the likes of Ian Locke again in her lifetime. So why was she walking away from him?

The town hall door opened and the twelve jurors followed the bailiff into the room and took their chairs. Some were grim-faced, but others appeared affable and relieved. Casey made an effort to catch the schoolmarm's eye. He acknowledged her with a slight nod of his head, and a faint trace of a friendly smile crossed his lips. Casey took this as a hopeful sign.

"Has the jury reached a verdict?" Judge Hutchens asked.

The blacksmith, who had been chosen by his fellow jurors as foreman, stood and replied, "We have, your Honor."

"And how find you?"

"The jury finds the defendant not guilty, your Honor."

Pandemonium broke loose in the courtroom. Casey turned to Celeste, who was smiling benignly but otherwise showed no emotion. "It's over," Casey said. "The judge will order you released in a few moments."

"I guess I should thank you."

Casey did not reply and began collecting her files and papers from the table.

"It is correct, is it not, that I can never be tried for this crime again?"

"You understand correctly. It's called double jeopardy."

"I did kill him you know. I did shoot the son of a bitch."

"I figured as much."

40

Ian

RAILROAD DEPOTS ARE fascinating places. I always like to arrive well before departure of a passenger train, not only because I am obsessively punctual, but also because I enjoy watching the people, scripting little stories in my head about where they are going, how they earn their livings, whom they love, what joys they have known, what tragedies they have suffered. This day, I would like to have been able to write my own story, or at least an ending to it. I guess that's what novelists do—play God with the lives of persons they create from their own imaginations. If I were a novelist, I suspect I would find myself constantly driven to resolve the drama in favor of a happy ending. But real life does not all that often, in my experience, bring happy endings. The most we can hope for is to balance defeats with victories.

Casey had purchased tickets for the only Saturday train to Omaha. A Denver & St. Joseph passenger car would be pulling out of Borderview at noon, carrying the woman who had bewitched me as no other ever had. I had hoped she might stay a few days following the verdict, but she had wasted no time making arrangements to shake herself free of Cottonwood

County. We had dined together at The Fremont the previous night, ostensibly to celebrate Casey's courtroom triumph, but it had not been an intimate occasion, for we were joined by Cam and Emily and even Mandy, who, despite a bruised and swollen face, was in good spirits and as enchanted with Casey as her father. They had forged a bond upon Mandy's escape from her ordeal that would be durable and lasting.

Casey had been politely good-humored and pleasant, laughing on occasion with some gusto at Cam's stories and anecdotes. My brother has a flair for turning the most somber occasion into a party and sometimes annoys me with his vetoes of any serious effort on my part to slip into a nice black mood. I believed Karl Wainwright when he told me Celeste had killed Ralph, and I found it difficult to rejoice at the freedom of a murderess. Not that it made any difference, but I wondered if Casey believed in her client's innocence. Intellectually, I accept the concept that guilt must be proven beyond reasonable doubt in a court of law, but viscerally I want to see the guilty punished. As a lawyer, I know my duty, but I accept fully that I am as much a hypocrite as any man.

I sat on a bench in front of the depot and studied the passers-by. Casey should arrive in a half hour. Mandy was helping Casey pack at the hotel, and they would say goodbye there. Cam was to meet Mandy and we would join up for lunch after the train departed. Cam had deftly negotiated Casey's departure arrangements so we might have some time alone, more or less, before the train left. Emily was to stay over till the first of the week when the new bank shareholders would meet. Cam and I had agreed that some shares in the Wainwright Savings Bank should be carved out for Emily, since as the sole heir to Ralph's insolvent estate her cooperation was critical to the bank's salvation. Emily, in turn, had asked me to establish a trust for Ralph's unborn child with part of her share.

I had promised Cam that Mandy and I would make a trip to the Kansas Flint Hills in a month or so, after I had the reorganization at the bank in place. Mandy should get acquainted with her grandfather and her cousins, Cam insisted, and I admitted a change of scenery for a spell might not hurt me. I had never seen any country more beautiful than the Flint Hills in the fall, with its scalped limestone ridges and sharply carved canyons painted by the multi-hued greens and browns of waning grasses and the ambers and crimsons of oak, ash, sumac and other trees and brush readying for winter. Yes, a brief change might help put a few things behind me.

"Hello, cowboy. Is this seat taken?"

Startled from my reverie, I looked up and saw a stunning redhead looking at me with mischievous green-flecked brown eyes. "You're early," I said, gesturing for her to take a seat beside me.

"I thought it would be nice if we had a little time together before I left. A young man from the hotel is loading my baggage on the train."

We sat on the bench watching the activity build up as departure time approached. I was glad to be with her and the silence was not an uncomfortable one. I just didn't know what more to say.

"Are you sorry?" she asked.

"About what?"

"About us. What happened between us."

"Never. How could I be sorry? Some folks go a lifetime

without having any real magic touch their lives. To be sorry would be to say I wished I hadn't experienced it." I took her hand but continued staring at the milling passengers, mere shadows passing in front of me now. "No, I'll take the magic when I can."

"It was an interesting idea," she said. "My reestablishing my practice here."

"I'm a realist, though. Your opportunities in the big city far exceed anything you could expect working from Borderview. I was advocating my own self-interest when I proposed a partnership."

She gave me a gentle nudge in the ribs with her elbow. "What would we have named such a partnership?"

I shrugged. "McGlaun, Heasty and Locke?"

"McGlaun first?"

"Ma'am," I said, "your bargaining leverage was overwhelming."

"Will you come to see me when you're in Omaha?"

"I'm welcome?"

"Of course."

"Then I'm sure we'll meet up again. But I need some time. Maybe a lot of it . . . to get over you."

The train whistle let out its mournful cry. The conductor called, "All aboard!"

We stood, and I walked her slowly to the passenger car. When we reached the boarding steps, she turned to me and looked up with tear-glazed eyes. She clutched me tightly, brushed her lips on my cheek and whispered, "I love you, Ian Locke. I'll love you the rest of my days."

Before I could reply, she disappeared onto the passenger coach, leaving me with my own words choking in my throat. I walked along the side of the coach trying desperately to catch one final glimpse, to give her a single last wave, but I could not find her.

The whistle gave its lonesome call again, and steam spewed from the engine. The racket of steel striking steel drowned out the other sounds as the train began to roll out of the station. I watched silently as the Denver & St. Joseph slowly moved Casey McGlaun, attorney at law, out of my life.

Then I heard a familiar voice call, "Ian! Ian!"

I looked up the track, perhaps twenty-five yards, and saw the billowing fabric of dresses fluttering off the side of the train and landing in small heaps along the side of the track. A huge carpetbag struck the depot platform and burst open, spilling and scattering the contents to the four winds. I raced along the track, and nearly out of breath, pulled even with the coach where Casey stood on the bottom entry step cheering me on. She leaped and landed with legs straddled around my waist and arms locked around my neck, before her momentum toppled us over and sent us rolling in the dust.

"McGlaun first," she said, as she pressed me to the earth and smothered my reply with her lips.

About the Author

Ron Schwab is the author of Night of the Coyote, Sioux Sunrise, Paint the Hills Red, and Last Will. He is a member of the Western Writers of America, Western Fictioneers, and Mystery Writers of America.

For more information about Ron Schwab and his books, visit the author's website at www.RonSchwabBooks.com.